ALL THE
RED ROSES

ALL THE RED ROSES

KATT CLOUATRE

iUniverse, Inc.
Bloomington

All the Red Roses

iUniverse books may be ordered through booksellers or by contacting:

iUniverse
1663 Liberty Drive
Bloomington, IN 47403
www.iuniverse.com
1-800-Authors (1-800-288-4677)

Because of the dynamic nature of the Internet, any web addresses or links contained in this book may have changed since publication and may no longer be valid. The views expressed in this work are solely those of the author and do not necessarily reflect the views of the publisher, and the publisher hereby disclaims any responsibility for them.

Any people depicted in stock imagery provided by Thinkstock are models, and such images are being used for illustrative purposes only.
Certain stock imagery © Thinkstock.

ISBN: 978-1-4759-3175-4 (sc)
ISBN: 978-1-4759-3176-1 (ebk)

Library of Congress Control Numver: 2012910870

Printed in the United States of America

iUniverse rev. date: 07/11/2012

CONTENTS

Dedicated to those, like me, who find a special refuge and quiet place in books that so many others can never seem to see. And especially to other undiscovered writers, young or old, no matter what genre. I learned the hard way that you can never really stop writing. It's always a piece of you. Never give up on the gift you've been given and find a way to share it with the world.

ACKNOWLEDGEMENTS

Mom and Dad: Thank you for teaching me that I can do anything I want to, teaching me right from wrong. More than anything, thank you for teaching me to never give up on the things you love most.

Aunt Sherry: Thank you for all the support you've given me. You were there from the very beginning offering ideas and creative criticism, pushing me and telling me to stop saying "if".

All my friends: Thanks for being there and letting me know that what I want and work hard for can become a reality. It's nice in such a different way to have friends tell you that would you do is worth doing, than having family tell you. It makes a special smile break out on your face that you never want to lose.

"Hope is the thing with feathers
That perches in the soul,
And sings the tune—without the words,
And never stops at all,

And sweetest in the gale is heard;
And sore must be the storm
That could abash the little bird
That kept so many warm.

I've heard it in the chillest land,
And on the strangest sea;
Yet, never, in extremity,
It asked a crumb of me."

—Emily Dickinson

TERRORS

"Father?" I called for him. If he did not wake soon he would be late for work. "Father?" I cracked his door open, hearing the sound of Mother scrambling eggs and setting out glasses of juice and milk. I let the heavy door swing wide. Father lay in bed as still as an infant. He did not move, not to roll over, or mumble at me . . . he didn't even breathe. I went up to his bedside shyly. He lie on his back, eyes closed and face lose. I touched his chest and cried out, "Mother, Mother!" My eyes were already burning.

My father's chest did not move with the air that should have been coming and going from his lungs. He should have been hot under the sheets but he was becoming cold without my mother's presence to keep him warm. His young heart should have beat strongly beneath his skin but there wasn't even a stutter. "What's wrong, Renee?"

"Father," I sobbed, "won't wake up!" I wouldn't admit to myself that he had been lost to us.

My mother put a soft hand on her husband, "Joseph?" He did not answer. My mother's eyes grew teary and she showed me out of the room. "Make sure your sister eats her breakfast. I'll be right back. I'm going to get Mr. and

Mrs. de Rosnel." I sat at the table and pushed a plate of eggs to Aria. I knew Mr. de Rosnel was a doctor. Father was ill . . . Father was dead. I also knew that the doctor's wife was Mother's closest friend. She would be there for Mother when the news was officially confirmed.

"What's going on, Reenie?" Aria called me by my nickname. She only called me Renee when she was serious. "Why is Mother so upset? Where's Father? He'll be late for work." She sipped at her orange juice and picked at her eggs.

"Mother is fine," I lied. "It's only her allergies again. Father won't be going to work today. He's too tired." My voice sounded stiff and automatic.

Mr. de Rosnel walked through the door and headed straight to Father's room. His wife and Mother followed him. "It'll be okay," she soothed my mother. She seemed to be the only thing keeping Mother from falling to pieces in front of us.

"What's wrong, Reenie?" Aria's voice was full of urgency now. She knew something was up when I didn't answer. "Renee!" she slammed her hand down on the table.

As I started to cry, she shook her head in denial and sprang from her chair, trying to run for Father's room. But I caught her, not wanting her to see him. "No!" she screamed, attracting the neighbors. "No, no, no!" I collapsed to the floor with her, crying out the tears that wouldn't stop—the tears that we *couldn't* stop. I heard Mother weeping then. Mr. de Rosnel walked by us slowly, looking down, not knowing what to say. He went out the door and explained to the crowd of people what tragedy had caused women to cry out as we had. I got up and walked away from all of the whispering and murmuring. I lay on the bed with Mother and Aria joined us.

Mother, in her pale blue gown, was draped across her late lover. As far as I knew Father and Mother had been in love since their times at school. We, in our pink and yellow gowns, lay next to her sobbing body. The bright colors blurred in my teary vision and Mrs. de Rosnel left the room, allowing us to mourn in private. No matter how bright our dresses were, they could not decorate my father's death. They became reminders of our distant happiness, like flowers upon a grave.

Eventually, our friends and relatives removed us from the body and took the shell that was father away. They would prepare him for the funeral. Already people were curious of how he died so suddenly . . . and we could not give an answer. We didn't know. All we knew was that the man of my mother's life—and Aria's and mine—was gone, and he was not coming back.

We cursed God and his ways. We cursed ourselves for no reason. We cursed Father for leaving us. At last we lay quiet and still, void of all emotion, taking refuge in our numbness.

That evening people came to our door once again, disregarding common courtesy. They asked us how a man like my father could have died. We still had no answer for them.

"We've seen your brews!"

"We've seen your potions!"

"A witch, you are!"

"How cruel, to poison a man like Joseph!"

"Witch!"

We shook our heads, "No, no. No such thing has occurred. We loved him." But the people had loved him too. They did not listen; they held us back as they took my mother by her hair and dragged her away as they shouted

3

impossible accusations. Our restrainers left us to join the crowd that was starting a fire ever so eagerly beneath our mother's bound feet. I could see the ropes that held her wrists and ankles were far too tight and cut into her fair skin.

We cloaked ourselves and ran to the crowd, but could not penetrate it. There was nothing we could have done for her. We couldn't even cry out to her. The people that did cry out were punished. "Sarah—" someone was bludgeoned in the head as she called out to my mother. "No!" someone was choked. The brave fools that tried to go to her were beaten down quickly and killed, leaving only the vile murderers behind.

My mother cried out as they lit the pile of dry wood on which she stood, "No, I'm no witch, please! Please!" her screeches pierced the coming night and made birds fly from their nesting spots. "God, oh dear God, help me!" Dogs barked on their chains; cats screeched and hissed in the back allies. "My children, no! Please, they need their mother! Please . . ." the heat of the fire was beginning to overwhelm her. That's when the flames began to lick at her feet. She tilted her head to the sky and groaned. Tears spilt down her ashen cheeks. She struggled against her bindings, causing the skin to break more and blood to slip across her fingers. All the while our old friends cheered on her agony.

They wanted her yells; they wanted her pain. They wanted her blood to boil and spill across the streets and bathe the town in a sinful red. The flames trickled up to blacken her legs and burnt her dress. She sobbed and screamed and choked. All Aria and I could do was watch. We knew we couldn't try to help her in anyway, but we couldn't take our eyes away from her death scene either. The fire sizzled her gorgeous brown hair and crept further up her body. Her face looked to the sky once more. But she did not yell, she did not beg. Our mother did not cry or plead.

Our mother looked to the heavens. The stars seemed brighter and closer and the moonlight cooled her face. Her eyes grew wide and clear. I know in my heart that she saw something that night, and I knew God was waiting at the gates for her along with Father. Slowly, her eyes rolled back and closed. Her chin fell to rest on her chest and finally her face was peaceful even as the fire caught hold of it and turned it forever black. Our mother's body was scorched and falling away; her clothes burned and clung to her body. Her prized hair was gone and the smell coming from her searing flesh was horrific. And still she was beautiful. No matter what those people did to her, that last bit that was left of her was not our mother. Mother was whole and well, resting somewhere where the light was warm and soft. She was safe.

My sister and I ran to our home, not knowing that it would be the last time it would ever be our home. We heard people coming about, "Kill the children! They have magic in their blood, too!" Aria and I looked at each other for an instant, all hope of crying through the night and having someone soothe us evaporated with the torch light that was nearing our home. All hope was lost with the insanity that overcame our town. We packed our bags hurriedly. I ran to father's room and threw all of his hard-earned money into a bag of dresses and then to the back of our home.

The first of the torches had been thrown into our home.

The first of the people were about to come through the front door.

With only precious seconds to spare Aria and I retreated out a back window. We ran, not knowing where we were going or where we would end up. At last we reached the harbor where a single ship was about to set out to sea. We ran towards it without thinking. Thinking would have only been a waste of time, it was our only chance.

We hid beneath deck and behind the crew's food, having to cup our hands over our mouths as men passed by us without notice. When we knew we were safely away from home we peaked out a crack of the wood of the ship. The fire light had reached the shore but no one seemed to shout for the boat to return. I let out a huge breath and cried silently. I knew we had just made the luckiest break of our life, but the way I could not help but see it then was the exact opposite.

Being burned would have been relatively quick. If we were discovered by the men a number of things could have happened. If we ate too much of their food they would have found us. If we were seen or heard or left a trail they would have found us. We could have been tossed into the icy black waters and left to drown slowly or die from exhaustion by trying to reach the shore. They could have killed us there on deck or used us as a punching bag. We could have become their little women pets and could have been subjected to any of their wishes.

At that point, I wished we had burnt with our mother.

RUNNING

The air was cold and the waters even more so, a slow, chill grave if we were caught. The sky out was a hazy orange lit by the evening sun, and clouds were hardly to be seen. I wanted to see the full of the sky more than anything in the world. I wanted to feel the warmth on my skin and have the sun's light fill me. I wanted nothing more than to hold the sun as I used to pretend I could. I wanted to stand on the very tips of my toes and raise my fingers to the heavens just to touch it.

Through another crack in the wood of the ship the land was getting ever nearer, our escape growing ever closer. The island grew out of the fog and shadows like an old memory.

I remembered the land from which I fled. The green fields and wooden houses that used to seem so sweet fell away from my mind. The kind smiles of my friends and family faded into darkness. Those happy memories had been replaced with nightmares of fire, death, and twisted faces. The people I once loved murdered my mother. Father had died. They had stripped everything from us. Those wretched people couldn't accept that another man, young and healthy and so in love, had passed without any reason. He'd not been murdered, nor had they found any trace of disease. So they called my mother a witch and claimed that she killed him while he slept. The events were still unfathomable to me.

As we sailed we'd seen hungry, green-eyed sea serpents and blue-eyed mermaids tempting the men to go to them and drown in the deep waters. There were huge man-eating fish that swam about the boat, too. We'd seen all of our childhood tales in that great sea while in hiding from the men on board, and we had agreed that we would trade them all for the stories of pixies and wood nymphs if we had the chance.

At times the silence and darkness we hid in were unbearable and I would've given anything to drown in that freezing ocean. I would have thrust myself into the dark waters and breathe in the salty water as if it were the most wonderful thing in the world. The only thing that kept me was Aria.

She was so young and scared and to leave her completely alone in this world would be absolutely cruel. So I stayed and now as we docked I could almost smell the fresh air, feel the solid earth beneath my booted feet. I could feel Aria squirming beside me, waiting to see the faces of people and hear any chat other than that of fish and water and women.

We longed to see the moon and the stars. We longed to see their silvery light on our skin and feel the cool breeze rustle our hair; hopefully it wouldn't be a breeze that smelled of sea salt.

"Be patient, Aria," I whispered. "We must wait 'til dark. If we leave now we'll be seen and this would all be for nothing."

She sighed so eager to be rid of the horrid smell of fish, eggs, pickles, and salted meats. "Where do you suppose we are, Reenie? We must be far away from Mar by now." I knew she was right. We had scratched lines into the ship's wood so we could keep track of the days, but we had to move our hiding place and lost count.

"I don't know. Wherever we are it has to be better. We'll make it better. As soon as we get out of here we'll rent a room with father's money and eat." My mouth watered for Mother's homemade cherry pie, roast beef, and mashed potatoes.

For the past month and more we had been forced to scavenge on fish and pickles and some of whatever we could get our hungry hands on. We lived like rats to go unnoticed.

We watched as the sky grew darker with every passing minute and when it was finally black with only the stars and moon above I crawled above deck first to check if anyone was still aboard. No one was and I knew all the men must be at a saloon drinking the past weeks . . . or months away. For the first time the deck was quiet of shouts and orders. There were no heavy footfalls and no pipe smoke.

The cool air brushed my face and the small breeze played with my long brown hair. Aria came on deck and seemed to almost cry when she saw the open space. We had both grown a little claustrophobic in the cramp spaces below deck.

"Let's get our things and leave. Be very quiet, we're not safe yet." So we did. When we scurried away from the ship we worried of how we would look in public. Our dresses were stained, torn and crumpled. I knew Aria's face was sallow and pale and I could only imagine what mine looked like. Our hair was tangled and our boots were dirty. We would look like horrid savages to all the suited men and silk-dressed women that rode in vehicles while we walked the streets in peasant-like wardrobe. We didn't even have a rag to clean our faces or a hat to cover them.

We would, without a doubt, be the laughing stocks of the city.

New Beginning

We came upon the lantern lit road and were awed to fit right in. The men wore trousers and suspenders with un-tucked, dirtied shirts. Their shoes were hardly more than shreds; their face hair grew unnoticed and they looked hard worked.

The women's dresses were as ours now looked: old, frayed and long used. Many wore hats upon their heads and mended shoes upon their feet. And their carriages! They didn't roll on their own! They were hooked up to huge groomed horses trotting to their destination; the ride looked quite bumpy and I pitied the one who had to clean the streets of what those horses left behind. Even the fine people that owned the carriages were dressed in plain suits and mere cotton dresses. They talked to the peasant folk as if they were all friends! No one noticed how odd this was and I didn't dare say a word.

No one looked at us suspiciously, not even with our carried bags and tired conditions. Most of the people here seemed to be tired and some carried their own bags in one direction or another. Most of those with bags went to a large wooden and stone building wedged between two others.

There was no hanging sign or label on the wall. There were hardly any signs to be seen at all. No cafes or theaters were noted. There wasn't even a sign that welcomed new comers into the city.

We followed a middle-aged man to the inn. It looked very humble but once inside it was a sort of heaven. No, there weren't gracious furnishings, crystal chandeliers, or expensive rugs. There weren't butlers in every corner or classical music being played in a corner.

It was still the best I could've dreamed for.

A great fire burned in a stone fireplace, warming the rooms and my weary bones. The chairs and tables were all wooden but looked fairly comfortable and candles and lanterns hung from the walls. There were many people talking, laughing and drinking in the small friendly room. A smell of pork and something else drifted to my defrosting nose. I was trying to figure out what the smell could be when a young maid came up to us. Her smile was bright and joyful. "Are you here to stay the night?" Her accent was strange and unplaceable.

"Yes. How much are the rooms?" I asked ready to pull out a handful of coins as I had seen Father do many times.

"Oh, you must not be from around here! I didn't think I recognized you," she giggled. "The rooms are 89 cent a night. If you want one of the really nice ones it's a little more. I think they're a dollar and 89 cent." I felt my eyes grow wide at their prices. "What's wrong?"

"Where we come from the rooms are quite a bit pricier. We'll take one of the cheaper ones, thank you." I handed her the few coins and she showed us to our room on the second floor. "Where is the bathing area?"

"All you do is heat up a bucket of water over the fire and poor it in the tub in the other little room. If you need some help carrying the bucket—'cause they get a little heavy—just find me and I can help you out. My name's Barbara," the girl added.

"Thank you," I said as I ducked into the room, hearing Aria murmur a thank you after me. She shut the door and the click of it closing reminded me of how much privacy meant to me. "It's a little small but it will have to do. We have to save every penny we can." I dropped my bags and lit a fire as Mother had taught me to do at home. Just to be indoors in this quaint, little warm room made my heart and soul sing. The bed was directly in front of us with a small table and window near the head. On the wall to my left was a small dresser and mirror with a tiny chair in front of it. To the right was a small fireplace and two buckets. The door on my right led to a small bathroom with—thank heavens!—plumbing. I'd been afraid we would have to use chamber pots.

But still, it wasn't much.

"Well, I'm not complaining," Aria plopped herself on the bed and removed her boots. "As long as it's warm and dry and there's a bed to sleep in with no ugly rats I am perfectly happy. Plus, there are no rough housing men standing just a few feet away from us." She wrinkled her nose in the disgust of a memory.

"Not to mention a chance to bathe." I set an already filled bucket of water on the hook over the fire to warm and took the spare bucket down to get more water. I passed a man coming up the stairs with his own bucket and he politely directed me to the back room of the inn where there was a water pump.

While waiting in line I watched people come in and out. Most of them would come in a foul mood but once they left, if they left, they would be grinning and laughing.

Most of the people were in their middle ages and the rest were around my age, nineteen. Most of the youth were work hands or in with their parents for a meal. They all knew each other and, even if they didn't like each other, there was a great amount of respect. In Mar I remembered how dislike for others were made well known and how it often led to a quarrel.

I filled my pail and had to carry it with both hands up the stairs. I was heaving when I finally poured the water into the tub and decided that I had just enough water. The hot water warmed my skin and muscles all the way down to my bones. I felt the dirt finally release from my hair and it felt so good I didn't move again until the water began to grow cold. By the time I had gotten off the ship I wouldn't have complained if I had to go jump in a river, as long as I could be clean.

I found Aria waiting in front of the fire trying to warm her toes through her thinned stockings. As she went down to fetch more water for herself I began emptying our bags into the small wooden dresser. After seeing our cloths in the light I decided to wash them all in the morning.

I was staring out our window when she returned. "Reenie, I have to say that I am quite a bit smarter than you tonight." I turned to see what on earth she could mean. "I found a nice young man that would help me while you had to suffer with your pails."

I took the bucket from the young man and poured it in the tub. "Well, maybe I didn't want to bother anyone. Everyone seems so busy." I nodded to the boy, "Thank you."

He bowed his head, sandy hair bouncing. "It was no trouble. A lady should not have to carry such a load. Goodnight, ladies. Sleep well." The blue-eyed boy bowed to each of us and left, gently swinging the door shut behind him.

"I think you are just too stubborn, Renee," Aria returned to our conversation as she went to bathe. "He was very handsome and kind. You have too much of Father in you."

"Maybe so but at least I wasn't flirting with the first man I met," even though Aria was only fourteen she had a severe interest in men. She was obviously growing interested in this one; no matter the fact he seemed to be a few years older than I was. "*You* have too much of Mother. You trust people far too easily and in our circumstances that can be a very dangerous game to play."

"At least I can trust, and I was not flirting! He asked me if I needed help, and I did."

"In times like these we shouldn't be too quick to trust, Aria. What if he was one of the shipmen or an officer? What if he was the town fool? Plus, I'm sure you played up how much help you required. You know you always do and I saw the way you batted your eyes at him!" I loved talking with Aria. We had always confused our simpleminded friends because we could keep up two parts of a conversation at once when they could hardly keep up with one. They would eventually give up listening and we'd giggle 'til our lungs wanted to burst.

"Okay, maybe I did play it up a little. Anyway, even if I did bat my eyes at him did you notice how he didn't seem to notice?" I almost laughed at the unconcealed hurt in her voice.

"I can't tell if he was being a proper gentleman or just being rude. I'd like to think that he was being a gentleman." She came and sat on the bed with me, clean but weary. "I know we shouldn't trust everyone we meet, but it's not like I told him anything just because he helped me fetch water. I'm not that naive." She sighed and rolled her eyes as she always did when she thought she was being underestimated.

"Fine, just be careful. As far as the boy goes he's far too old for you anyway, you know Mother would never approve." I waited for her response, but when I rolled over she was already asleep under the covers. I crawled under them and as I stared into the dying fire light I drifted to sleep just as quickly as sweet Aria had.

I knew when I woke in the warm daylight that I had not slept peacefully, though it seemed that my sister had. I had a dream. It must've been very strange because I remember there being magic and fire. Other than that I remember nothing. Maybe I had just dreamt of an old bedtime story Mother once told me.

I discarded the nightmare, knowing it was only caused by stress and fatigue. I crawled out of bed to not disturb Aria and went down to fetch water for clothes. When I went down the workers seemed to be half-asleep themselves and I caught sight of the boy from last night sleepily but steadily sweeping the floor. His broom swayed slowly back and forth to the rhythm of a water drip somewhere in the kitchen.

As I pumped the water I wondered how long he had to work into the night. I shook my head. It wasn't my concern and it was his job. Father often had to work much later than he wished to and still got up at his usual time.

There was an endless stream of clothes to wash and I eventually woke Aria to help. We drowsily cleaned and laid the garments out to dry. Aria was humming a tune my father had played on the fiddle and stared out the window. No doubt she was eager to explore. I turned to my thoughts for comfort.

For a strange reason I could smell Mother's tea. It was a special tea she gave to people when they were sick. The stuff tasted absolutely horrific but by the next day you felt better. I remembered her putting a blue jay feather under my pillow at night when I had a toothache or a headache. Mother had all sorts of remedies for such things. Father had always said that it was just in our heads, that since we believed we would feel better, we did. Mother would chuckle when he left. She always told us that certain things in life could remedy others.

Looking back, I realized that such concoctions could be called a witch's brew. Yet, the town had not retaliated. No, many women in town had strange cures for every which thing. Mother didn't have the heart of a witch, much less the warty nose.

There was a knocking on the door, "Breakfast is being cooked if you'd like to come down and get some!" It sounded like that Barbara girl. I wanted to get a good look at her and all the other people in the light. They had felt so unreal last night. They had felt like shadow-ghosts from a dream and I wasn't sure if I was imagining them or not.

Aria hung the last of the laundry. "Let's go, I'm starving!" I laughed and followed her out the room with some money in my dress pocket. "Their food smells funny, but a good kind of funny." She stopped suddenly on the stairs and turned, almost making me walk right over her. "You know, we still have no clue as to where we are. I haven't seen a sign or heard a name or anything. This place is so very strange, Reenie. I don't understand it."

"I'm sure Barbara will tell us. As long as it's not a ship I really don't care!" We both giggled as we headed down the stairs. We sat at the bar reading the small menus.

They had strange things to eat. In Mar we had pork and beef, roast and chicken. Of course, they did too, but they had things I had never heard of before. They had Sausage, Bear, and Wild Boar. One of the waitresses passed and I asked. "I'm sorry but I don't know what some of this is."

The old blonde smiled at me, "You're not from around here are you, sweetie?" We shook our heads. "Sausage is just a long round piece of meat that you can cook and slice up. A wild boar is just a big wild pig; bear is just this big animal. I guess it looks like a dog, but then again it doesn't; I just know that it's real good, Miss." She looked at our confused faces and giggled, "We do have scrambled eggs, toast and bacon, too."

"That would be great," Aria smiled back with a sigh of relief.

"So where are you girls from, anyway? You wouldn't happen to be from Crick, would you?" The older blond woman asked. For some reason she looked very familiar.

"No, ma'am," I answered. "We're from Mar."

"Mar? How'd you get way over here? Roe is half a sea away. No! Don't answer that. It's not my business. I hope you like it here." She smiled wide. "I'll be right back with your breakfast."

The city of Roe. We had sailed to an island in the middle of the sea! Father had shown of many maps of the world. One day he placed his finger on a small speck. "That's where I went during my last business trip girls: Traper. It's a small island, see?" We nodded and he continued. "In the next century the sea will most likely claim it," he smiled at Mother Nature's ways. "On the southern side it was beautiful and the people were kind. Much of it is still farm land though. These squiggly lines are mountains and valleys. The natives said they stretch from one end of the island to another. They told me it was treacherous and filled with strange creatures, so no one ever crosses to the north. We sailed around to the northern side," he traced the coast line with a finger, "and there was a large town called Roe. There were many pastures and small roads that must have led to other towns." He hesitated for a moment. "But in this city . . . the people were strange." He had left it at that for us to wonder.

"Roe," Aria tested the name on her tongue. "So that's where we are. Didn't Father do business here before?"

"Yes. He said it was awful and filled with dark magic, but I can't believe he was talking about this place. Everyone seems in such good spirits." The people were happy. I hadn't seen so much as a small quarrel. "Thank you," I told the woman when she brought our food.

She turned her head about the room seeming to look for someone that was not to be found. "Where are your parents, girls?"

I didn't even hesitate, "They passed away recently and we have no other family. We came here to start anew." I swallowed some delicious eggs and continued. "I think our feet led us to the right place. It's very nice here," I lied. Lying felt like the right thing to do for the moment. Starting off with getting pity from someone is never the way to go; and it wasn't as if some mysterious feeling led us here. We jumped at the first chance to escape death, just as anyone else would have.

"It's good you think so. What a pity, though. They must have still been young. Well, if you need anything, anything at all, you just find me. I'm Barbara's mother. Call me Chene." No wonder she looked so familiar. They shared large dimples, a toothy grin and that dark blonde hair.

"Well, Chene," Aria pushed away her empty plate, "we must be going. We would like to look around the town for a little while. All we've seen in good light is the inside of this inn." We smiled and waved to her. When we walked out the door onto the stone streets it was very much alive.

Carriages passed carriages as whinnies filled the air, mixed with the sound of rolling, bouncy wheels. Young children held their mother's hands as they walked in the bustling streets. Older children ran on the side, dodging in and out of doorways, giggling on their way. Men walked to work in their tattered shoes and battered hats. Maids swept dust from their doorways and shooed away the kids, fussing about trouble and chaos. Others beat out laundry from their high windows seeming to be hard working princesses in their lovely dungeon towers.

Down a ways to the left there was a lively market and we made our way to it in the constant flow of commoners. There were strange red fruits with green leaves like hats on their tops. I heard an old lady call them strawberries. We didn't have those in Mar. They had other strange fruits. Some were yellow, others green, and others even strangely shaped and purple.

Their sweets smelled heavenly. They had pies of all sorts and jams to match. They had cakes and muffins galore that tempted my nose with their sugary scent.

"Oh I'm so excited," we heard one woman rave on and on. "The parade is coming up and my young Sandra is one of the New! Her Father and I are so proud." Many people, now that I actually listened, shrilled over a festival and some New people.

"That must be why everyone is in such a good mood. I wonder what they're celebrating," I said thoughtfully. We wondered the road a little longer. We peaked into bakeries and clothing shacks. When we found a library we slipped into the musty room. It was fully stocked and many children were packed in groups seeming to dream for what lay in the books' pages.

I ran my fingers across the spines of leather bound books and read the strange fantasy names. There were books like *Sorcerers' Spells*, *Bringing Back the Dead*, *Spirits*, and one very old, thick novel, *Maria Lenark*. It had an aura about it that told you to handle it with the utmost of care.

We exited the library and started back to the inn. Beyond the city I could see where the road was no longer stone, but simply dirt. Houses lay on hills and acres of livestock and farmland lay open in the sun. I could see the mountains that no sane person would cross. I imagined trees and fog and unruly beasts hiding in the valleys and rivers there.

Aria interrupted my thoughts, "We have to ask someone what the celebrations are about. Maybe we could ask Barbara or Chene. I'm sure they would be happy to tell us."

"Most likely," I agreed with my little sister, admitting to myself that curiosity was nagging at me as much as it was Aria. "Aria, why do you suppose the library had so many fairytales? Who is Maria Lenark? This place seems a bit strange, kind of like those happy places in stories Mother used to tell us but all the happiness was just a show."

"You have an imagination like Mother's. Aren't you happy during a celebration? Like Christmas or Valentine's Day? I'm sure that's just what's going around here."

"Yes. Perhaps you're right," I laughed. It was probably just my imagination.

Aria just nodded. "I don't know. Maybe it's just a library for kids as ours had separate sections," she offered an answer to my question. "The grown up one couldn't have been too far. As for that Maria woman, we could ask Barbara that, too. She probably grew up reading that book. It looked old enough for her mother to have read it, too."

Maria Lenark

We walked into the inn and hardly recognized it. Most of the guests had been shooed out or up to their rooms to make way for the busy workers. All of the hands were scurrying about, hanging tassels and ribbons in every corner and placing decorated candles on every cleared surface. Flower petals were strewn about the unlit candles and wind chimes hung above our heads.

Most of them were made of crystal or glass and the rest were made of a shining metal. They tossed rainbow light here and there across the floors and walls and made sweet tinkling sounds that reminded me of the songs of morning birds. Maids were scrubbing floors and counters spotless, and from the kitchen and the back we could hear the clattering of a feast being prepared. Aria looked about, "They must be decorating for the parade tomorrow."

We walked to the back where the water pump was to find the boy from last night cleaning dishes. He nodded politely to us and returned to his work. "What will the town be celebrating?" I questioned him, feeling as if I wasn't right to interrupt his work.

Without glancing up from his chore, "It's the Crystal Moon Parade." When we said nothing he went on to explain. "Tomorrow night is the night where the moon looks glassy like crystal and everyone says that magic is in the air and easiest to reach. The magic workers walk through the streets in colorful robes holding decorated candles. A group of children walk among them dressed in all white carrying white candles. The white represents the blank page their life is, like an unwritten book. They are the New."

"What's so special about the New?" Aria asked.

"The New are youth that recently discovered their ability to harness the world's energy. Tonight we celebrate their new journey into the world of magic." He scrubbed his dishes and dried them routinely, keeping his voice flat and void.

"Magic," I thought of my mother, falsely burnt at the stake for it. "You mean this place is packed with witches?"

"Yeah," he acted as if this was all normal. "Not the type of witches you're thinking of. The magic workers here use things like remedies for illnesses; keeping birds away from crops, helping a woman in labor, things like that. Only a few use black magic and those use it carefully as not to get caught. Most of the spells in the library are ones used to help. It's not as if we're all using voodoo dolls or something." He laughed and looked up from his spot on the floor. I knew that behind those painstakingly blue eyes he was thinking that I expected witches to disgusting old hags that cursed men . . . and he was right.

"So you're a witch," I had to keep myself from taking a step back and I saw Aria bite her lip. "Everyone here is a witch?"

"Not everyone, of course. If everyone was there would be many quarrels for power and respect. As for myself, I can do very little." I could tell he was lying. "Chene's grandmother was a very powerful witch, curing the sea plague with teas and soups and a few loose ends; but you've seen Barbara. She doesn't have hardly a lick of it in her." He stood and stretched his long legs.

"So those books in the library are all real? Wow," Aria breathed. Her eyes narrowed slightly with a forgotten thought only now resurrected to her memory. "Who is Maria Lenark? Was she a witch?"

"You don't know much at all about this place, do you? Let's go sit at a table," he suggested.

He ordered us a pitcher of cider and after taking a sip he started, "Yes, Maria Lenark was a witch. She was the most powerful we know of. The things she could do were great, some absolutely horrid, but great nonetheless."

"What could she do?" Aria whispered, completely enticed in Maria's legendary tale. "What was she like?"

"Well, she was a woman of mixed skin and an old family. She was very beautiful and drew men to her like flies to honey," his eyes were on me as he said this and I struggled not to fidget. "If a man she wanted did not come she would put a spell on him to make him adore her. If that didn't work she disposed of him." He nodded at Aria's gasp.

"She was a woman that knew what she wanted and got it or no one did. When she got angry she could conjure a storm of great destruction, and when her spirits were high the sun could be out and roses could grow in the depth of winter if she wished it. Maria was a master of black magic. She kept a stock of voodoo dolls and pins; she kept chicken heads to cause sicknesses, scattered crow feathers to cause bad luck for whomever she had in mind.

"Despite all of her madness she was well liked. She was great with the town kids. She would spark fire from her hands and make pebbles disappear and return them from behind their ears. She brewed stews to heal and roasted seeds in molasses for good luck and all the women envied her garden. Maria's garden was glorious and vibrant. She could make anything grow and make a weed look as beautiful as a rose."

For a moment he looked very thoughtful, "You know . . . she never would plant a red rose in her garden. She had yellow roses, and white, pink, and starburst. But not a single rose was red. People say she said that red roses were a sign of passion, but passion can come in many forms. Depending on why one is given a red rose it could mean unimaginable love . . . or hatred so fiery it can burn one's soul." He grew silent and drank his cider.

I thought about Maria. She was like a coin. On one side she was an evil cold-hearted hag while on the other side she was a ray of sunshine and a breath of fresh air. "What happened to her?" I asked, almost scared to receive the answer.

The boy, I still didn't know his name, looked up from his glass. "She died," he said matter-of-factly.

"Yes, but how? Was she burned at the stake or drowned?"

"No, not even close. Her death wasn't that peaceful. She was murdered by her own son. She knew that her use of black magic was wrong but she also knew how to balance it with good. She saw her son fading more and more into the shadows, unashamed. She saw him becoming a monster." Though his story was touching and heart breaking, I felt as if sarcasm slipped into his words now and then. "She had to do something, so she tried to put a purifying potion in his wine one night but he could smell it. He grew very angry and wouldn't listen to his mother's pleas to find balance and to stop his nonsense. He grabbed a kitchen knife and slashed at her, but thanks to her foresight she ran in time. She ran into her garden where she had always felt safe and protected by the sweet fragile fragrances of a hundred soft flowers. He killed her there, in her own sanctuary."

As he spoke I could see poor Maria, as I'm sure Aria could too. I could see her trying to help her no-good son, unwilling to use her magic against him. And he had killed her.

"The townspeople found her that morning and her blood had already soaked into the roots of her bright roses. They drug Samuel, the traitor son, from his house and hanged him in the tallest oak. It's said that they let his body hang there in honor of Maria. He wasn't cut down until four days later when his mother had been properly mourned and buried and her grave covered with white roses and daffodils.

"On the fifth day an omen came to the people that Samuel may be dead, but he was far from gone," the boy's eyes grew dark and grave. "As a sign of his evil spirit lingering Maria's roses started to fade from their rainbow of colors and all shade into a ghastly red. They were blood red. But . . . one rose, one tiny, young rose, remained white. Maria would stay as long as her son did—she would fight his black magic with her good and serve as a light in the darkness."

We were all quiet for a long time sipping our cider and staring at nothing in particular. "Is it all true? About Maria and Samuel? And the roses?" Aria asked.

"Tomorrow, follow the parade of people. They will prove it to you. We all march to Maria's old house and the very garden where her soul left her body to wonder, forever earthbound. The house is as it was those many, many, many

27

years ago . . . and so is her garden; blood red roses still grow there along with a single white rose. We honor her there with silence."

"I don't know if I can believe all of this. Ghosts and magic are parts of bedtime stories, not true life," Aria stated, shaking her head.

"I don't know. Can't you feel it? Everything seems so heavy here, weighed with some power," I said. I had no idea where these words had come from but they just felt right. The boy smiled at me the dimming daylight. That smile made my heart pound and my knees weak.

"Harro! Don't be scaring the guests or giving away the goods! Now, come help finish cleaning up!" Chene hollered from the kitchen. "And light those candles while you're out there!"

The man, Harro, bowed to my sister and me. "I hope to see you later, ladies," he said as he waved his arm around the room. As he did so, the candles lit suddenly, flames licking where moments ago there had been merely shadowed space. I gasped at his use of magic and he winked at me and walked away to the kitchen with a flourish.

My stomach preformed back flips in my body, and not just because of how nervous the use of magic had made me.

I stared after him in wonder then to the burning candles. Aria's mouth hung loosely and she ran up to our room with tears in her eyes.

I stood and watched as a child looked nervously at one of the many candles. Her friend put his fingers over the flame and swiftly pulled them back. Strangely, though his hand had been slightly seared by the heat of the flame, he only let it drop by his side with a sad, disappointed look upon his tiny face. Children could be so silly; of course the fire would hurt.

The little girl looked at him smugly and thrust her hand into the fire. She held it still and let the flames lick at her fingers. When she pulled it from the fire it held no sign of the awful burn that should've been there. I could only assume that she was one of the New, using her power to elude the heat. She was proud and full of triumph. I would have been happy to be the boy, no powers. I was like the boy, I had no worries over that, but he looked sad.

BLIND DECISIONS

I shook my head and followed the stairway to where my sister had retreated. "What's wrong?" I asked her small, curled up, sobbing form.

She looked up from her pitiful pool of tears. "What do you mean 'what's wrong?'!" she screamed. "Mother died because of what he could do! Yet here they celebrate it and witches are *honored*! She was burned *alive*! If only we had been here. She wouldn't have been touched! Here it wouldn't have mattered if she used magic or not! She would still be alive!" her sad tears turned into a blind rage and fizzled into misery and exhaustion.

I wrapped my arms around her small frame as she carried on. "Why did they do it? How could they even think of it?" she choked a little between words and silent tears spilt from my eyes now. I rocked her until she fell into a fitful, dreamless sleep. She was right. Here was a haven for most people. Mar was a land of the norm; now a land of the cruel and the dead . . . but that was normal now.

I dried my eyes and closed the door softly. At the bottom of the stairs a voice called to me, "I'm sorry for upsetting your sister. I only meant to entertain."

It was Harro, the only one in the room. His blond hair and blue eyes flickered in the glow of the firelight. The red light that covered him was eerie. He stretched lazily in an old wooden chair. He seemed a perfectly content, wondrous spectacle, like my kitten back home when she sprawled out in a sunny spot. He could've been an angel painted by a great master.

I could only imagine what I looked like. Wretchedly pale, even in the glow? Brown hair like a bird's nest and the color of trees? Brown eyes looking as black as a demon's in the shadows? I must've been a hideous sight to behold.

I sat in a chair near him. "It's not your fault. There are just sensitive matters in our family right now." Harro stared at me curiously. I didn't know if I should tell him or not but his deep brooding eyes prompted me.

"In Mar our mother was accused of being a witch when our young father mysteriously died. We watched her burn and people cheered for her cries of pain," my voice was low and fragile. "She was killed for the very thing you hold with the highest respect here. It upset us both a little to see someone use magic with humor."

"I'm sorry. Truly," he said softly. We sat in silence, lingering in our own thoughts, or perhaps just enjoying a moment when no thoughts came to mind.

"Would you like to go somewhere with me?" he asked lightly. "It's just down the street and I think you'd love their food. The inn is nice but eating from the same menu all the time, as I have, gets tiring and bland." He smiled broadly and tempted me with his eyes. He stood and offered me his arm. I got up from my chair smiling timidly and took it as he led me out the door.

I had let my hand rest lightly around his arm, trying not to show that touching him made me nervous. If he noticed it he thought it amusing because he said nothing about it.

The appearance of the town still took my breath away. Lanterns were hung outside of doors to light the way. Lovers walked slowly by holding hands. Young kids were being called in for supper and bed while others walked far from their homes and back again. The little market that we had visited earlier was dark and abandoned since at this time of evening people preferred the warmth and comfort of their homes. They preferred to spend it with their families indoors or eating somewhere or telling stories by the fire. Dogs took a rest from their chase of the cats that sat high above on window seals that they could never reach. Cats departed from their mission to shed and beg to be rubbed. Less and less phaetons passed on the road.

Harro directed me up the street. "I'm very glad you came here."

"Why? All the people here seem happy and know everyone. I expect you would have many friends and a family," I reasoned. "The appearance of one person could not have made that much of a difference."

He shook his head, "I don't have that many friends—I don't have any, really. I'm still kind of new here and this town has been of the same families for generations. I can understand that it must be hard for them to accept someone new, but still. And since I moved here I have no family here. I do get rather lonely at times."

"Well, I *suppose* I could be your friend," I joked. "You know I'm an outsider, too. I have to say that even back home it got lonely. I guess I can understand how one person could make a difference in a person's life."

"Especially, when that person happens to be a fair, young maiden," he smiled. I looked down, embarrassed by his not so concealed compliment. "Do not be embarrassed, Renee. You are very beautiful and kind to a lonely stranger."

I could feel his eyes on me but I could not yet meet his gaze. I was lucky that it was gloomy enough out that the shadows hid my deep blush. If he noticed I would have only blushed cherry red.

"Here we are." He indicated an old wooden shop that glowed with a soft yellow light. He opened the door for me and a little bell tinkled cheerfully. We sat at a table and a nice waitress came by. "Tea and a rugan cake for the both of us," he told her. "Trust me you'll love it. Their tea is the best I've ever had."

"What is the rugan cake like?" I asked, imagining the worst thing possible. I don't even know what I was thinking of; the picture in my head was just a clunk of muck on a plate.

"It's excellent. It has cream and icing and cherries. There are chocolate chips in it and a center of fudge. It's very sweet but once you have a bite you couldn't stop even if you wanted to." He leaned towards me with his elbows on the table.

"Harro," I began curiously, "what made you decide to come here if you knew that you wouldn't be that easily accepted? I mean, it's a nice place and all, but I could've thought of so many other places to go." I could tell my question had caught him off guard.

"Well, I don't know if you could understand, not being a witch," he nodded at the waitress and took a bite of his cake. I poked mine with a fork; it looked pretty good.

"I seem to find that I am always underestimated. Try me. If I don't understand then I won't keep on," I took a sip of my tea, refusing to let myself jump when it burned my tongue.

He smiled and I blushed again, but not so heavily. "Where I was, people started to guess at what I am. You witnessed yourself what happens to people who are condemned of being a witch. So I moved here. I knew that I wouldn't be forced out here or threatened. In a way I would be accepted. I wouldn't have to face the gallows or the stake here. Even if I am not considered one of them I can still call this place my home and sanctuary."

"That wasn't very hard to understand," I bit into the rich cake. It wasn't all he said it would be, but it was still good. "It must be a woman thing. All men underestimate women."

"Particularly beautiful women," he smiled. I rolled my eyes, already tiring of his game.

"Why do you do that?" he asked pointing at my face. "Why do you blow off any sign of affection or adoration?"

"I've already seen many girls here that are far more beautiful than I am. I know that I am plain," I had accepted this fact long ago.

"True again," Harro said and, even though I had just said so, his agreement hurt a little. "There are some girls here that I wouldn't mind taking back to my quarters after a hard day of work, but they are empty inside. Sure, they are pretty on the outside, but on the inside they are vain, shallow and clingy. I prefer headstrong women, ones that take a little convincing. I like it when a lady has an air of respect about her and a head on her shoulders. It's easier to converse but at the same time much more challenging to catch her," he looked at me. "I like a challenge." He smiled a crooked smile and I blushed deeply; this time I was not lucky enough to have the gloom to shadow my face.

Mother had always said that I would never find a man because of my strong will and stubbornness. Yet, here was one that looked for exactly that in his other half. I had to stop; I couldn't let my head get too big over this boy. We ate and drank in silence for a while.

I wished I could look ahead and see what the future held in store for Harro and me. It would be such a relief to know if it was worth wasting my time on him or if it would all be for not. Would Harro and I even have a future together? Would it be good and happy? Would it be sad and painful? Life was so confusing. Why does it have to be so difficult?

I looked out the window to see Aria pass in a group of people. The girls seemed curious of her. She mainly ignored them and focused all of her attention on entrancing the young men in the group. She looked like she was doing a good job at it. They were bug-eyed and red-faced. Their lips moved in stutters as she batted her long lashes at them. She had always been such a flirt and I knew she wouldn't change until the day she found a husband. Even then, I would imagine that she would constantly test the patience of her husband. She passed by, all the while flirting unabashed. I laughed.

"For that, I do envy your sister. If you were more like her, socially, we would be *very* good friends by now. Then again, I would have to compete with every man in the city and I don't know how long I would last against some of them," Harro laughed.

I snorted at him. "Oops," I giggled. My hand had hit my cake and I had a small smear of fudge across my knuckles. I was just about to wipe it off when Harro took my hand. He kissed away a dab of the chocolate. He looked up and slowly did the same to the rest. He smiled mischievously as I retrieved my hand.

He was what Mother called a bad boy. He didn't go around being outlandish but he was very outgoing. She had told me that Father had been one and her heart had squeezed until she couldn't breathe. Only now did I truly understand what she meant.

We finished eating without a word. When I was done he stood behind me and pulled out my chair. He took my hand as we walked into the cool night air, and when I shivered he wrapped his arm around me. I was afraid to lean into him. That would mean that I liked him back and I wasn't sure if I did or not yet. Well, I was very sure I liked him; I just wasn't sure if that was a good or bad thing yet.

We walked in the empty streets. It was so quiet that I could hear a cat meow from a rooftop and the tinkle of a bell sounded as if was right next to me. Our feet thudded loudly on the cold stones and whispered through the leaves. It was so quiet I could hear Harro's deep breathing and the slow steady thrum of his heart from deep within his large chest. The longer we walked shoulder to shoulder the more I could feel the beat of his heart in his veins. His presence warmed me like a soft blanket. "I hope you choose to stay here for a while, Renee," he said simply.

"I think I will. The people here are especially nice," I smiled. He held me a little tighter. As strange as it was, he liked me. I was a plain girl. I had thick brown hair and unimpressive brown eyes. I was only of average height. I was orphaned and on the run.

Strange as it was, he liked me. He was a blond-haired, blue-eyed angel. He was tall and strong. He was beautiful in every way. His very voice could make a weaker woman swoon. His smile lit the night and overpowered the sun. His strong hands were ever so gentle with me as if I was a precious glass figurine. Yet, as strange as it was, he adored me.

I wanted very much to return his affections, but I wasn't ready. I was still getting over the loss of Mother and Father. I had to get over the loss of all of my friends and everything I knew; everything I once held dear. I had to take on the responsibility of Aria. I had to figure things out before I could move on and there were still too many things to figure out.

We were nearing the inn and Harro let the arm he had wrapped around me fall to his side. Such uncommitted affections were not meant to be shown in public so I took his arm once again. I could show him that much. He led me into the weary inn. At the end of the stairs he took my hand and kissed it politely, "Good night, my lady." He bowed and walked to the kitchen. I was so giddy I practically danced up the stairs.

DREAMS AND DREAMERS

I was humming a tune when I walked through the door. I laughed at the sight of Aria. She lay on her stomach, her legs kicking in the air. "What are you doing?"

She waved her hand at the four roses set in front of her. They were all different colors: white, yellow, pink and blue. Not a single one of them was a red rose. "I'm trying to decide. They're all so sweet and courteous! Not to mention how down right, drop dead gorgeous they were! Except for Marcus, he still had a little boyish cuteness in his face. It made him look just a little too young, but he was the most romantic. Life is hard," she sighed contentedly. "I saw you and Sir Harro. You two make such a good couple."

I plopped down next to her, "We are not a couple—"

"Yet."

"No, not yet," I smiled. "He was just showing me a good time; being polite, you know. I do think he likes me. I think he likes me a lot, but as you said: I have too much of Father in me. I don't trust him enough yet to make it official. I mean, we've only just arrived and I already have a suitor? No, that screams desperate."

"You could always take a hint or two from me. I have four suitors currently," she lifted her brows at me.

"You treat your men as you treat toys. They entertain you for a while but when a shiny, new one comes along you cast that one away. Your men all have an expiration date on them. I'd like something more mature and romantic, if you don't mind. Plus, I don't think Harro is the type that would be just thrown away to make room for my next . . . What did Anna call it? A boy toy? Yes, Harro is not a boy toy, Aria. Once I get to know him a little more I think I might fall for him." I giggled with excitement.

I'd been vexed by other boys before, but they never lasted long. They were all in the mood for an unintelligent woman who kept her mouth shut and her legs open, and I was the exact opposite. Harro was different, special. He was the perfect fit for me so far but a part of me told me that he was dangerous and should be handled with caution. All men could be dangerous so I cast that thought away and slept.

I dreamt that it was snowing out and the town was empty. I walked through the fluffy snow clothed in my warmest attire. I could hear my boots crunch in the white blanket. The air was so quiet and dense that my footsteps echoed loudly in the cold. My breath formed crystals in the chill air and my nose burned with the cold. I should've been scared to walk alone in cold deserted streets but I wasn't. I knew I was in no such danger; I could tell it was all just a dream.

I kept on walking and the snow kept falling at an unusually steady pace, a pace that only exists in dreams like this. It fell in small little packs that reminded me of a little bit of heaven. It was so white it could've been from an angels glow. I ventured on into a small courtyard. The little well in the center was piled up with snow and the roof had fallen in. I heard foot crunches behind me and turned.

It was sweet Harro. He stood out against the pale fluff, dressed in all black. It must've been one of those dreams were you can't talk because I remained silent even though I wanted to ask him what he was doing here in my dream. He stepped towards me and I smiled. He smiled too and made his way to me until he was barely a foot away. He stared into my eyes and cocked his head curiously. Slowly his face approached mine, both of our eyes closing. Strangely, I could still see what was going on. 'I must being seeing my dream in third person,' I thought.

His warm lips met mine as softly as a dove's wing. His kiss was sweeter than the rugan cake he had bought me. I could feel all his love and emotions, as I know he could feel mine. He held my face in one hand and kissed me 'til the end of the world and heaven and earth melted together. He kissed me until the whole world consisted of just the two of us and the heavens turned to night and fire rained down on us.

His hand tightened on my jaw. Quickly, it grew to be an unbearable pain but I couldn't scream out for him to stop. His lips left mine and he held my throat in two skeletal hands now. He was choking me. I knew my lungs were begging for air but it was a dream and I was numb to this fake pain. Slowly, ever so slowly, Harro's beautiful face twisted and deformed itself. I soon found myself staring into Samuel's cold black eyes. As soon as I knew my dream-self was dying I was falling in to the well. He stared down at me, satisfied as I fell to my death.

I shot up in bed sweating. Aria groaned and rolled over, still in her sleep. I kept telling myself that it was only a dream, as I knew it was, but I couldn't go back to sleep.

How did I know what Samuel would look like? Why would I have such a dream?

I just had to wait it out until morning. I prayed that it would not be snowing when the sun lit the world. If it was I might go crazy. I simply laid there for hours watching my sister toss and turn. She would throw her covers off then yank them back to her. I knew it was wrong to do so but I took refuge in the fact that she wasn't sleeping well either. It was nice to know that someone else suffered with me. At last I couldn't just lie there anymore and I knew that I would drive myself insane if I paced. I got up and put the bucket of water over the fire. I teased the fire with straw and more wood until it blazed out of the embers. I took the other bucket in my hand and slowly plodded down the stairway. I was careful as not to make a sound. Waking up twenty other people would not be in my best interest right now. I felt my way to the back where the water pump was. Sadly, I could not quiet that old thing. I gritted my teeth as the rusty metal creaked.

When the bucket was finally full I grabbed it and turned only to squeal at the sight of Harro. "Don't scare me like that!" I whispered roughly as I clutched my chest. My heart had jumped and started pounding like crazy. "How long have you been standing there?"

He shrugged, "A few moments, I suppose. Not that long." He leaned on the wall, blocking my path. "Let me help you." He took the pail from me and followed me up to my room. I hoped Aria hadn't woken up. I just knew she would make all sorts of crazy accusations if she saw Harro in our quarters in the middle of the night. I put my finger over my lips before walking through the door and he nodded. He put the cold bucket over the fire and then poured the boiling water into the tub for me.

I mouthed a thank you to him and expected him to leave. He only nodded curtly and put his fingers under my chin. He lifted my face to his and I felt his lips curl upward against mine. He pulled back to look at me and I felt myself blush.

I was entirely sure that I liked him now. My heart beat rapidly in my chest and my throat squeezed in time with my stomach.

He hugged me tightly and kissed me again. His hand tightened on my waist and his other traveled down from my chin to brush my shoulder. I pushed away from his embrace. I made my eyes grow big and nod toward the room where Aria was still sleeping. I wanted to say, *You can't be serious. Aria is right there.* The only reason I didn't say it out loud was for my fear that Aria would wake at the slightest noise.

He gave me a crooked smile and clutched my hands in his eagerly. He whispered very softly, "Come back to my room with me." My eyes grew bigger and my jaw dropped at his bluntness. "Come," he urged me with a face that was so sexually convincing that I almost did. My face grew stern and serious, and a little scared. I shook my head and pointed to the door as if to say, *Leave now.* He smiled again and slowly walked out of my room like a cat; so calm and relaxed in his stride, as if he had made no attempt to bring me back to his room and have me for the night.

I locked the door behind him.

At last I crawled in the warm bath water and felt my muscles relax from the fright of my dream and stress of Harro's abruptness. I was never meant to have to go through all of this. I didn't like not knowing people or what was going on or what would happen. If everything had went on as it had been I could've told you how my life would have played out. I would have had to put up with Aria's taunting when she was proposed to before I was. Mother and Father would be frantic, then everything would calm down again. Taylor would have asked for my hand and I would have said yes. We would have had a splendid wedding and a romantic honeymoon. We would get our own house near town and fill it with love and happiness. We would have had many children and would have watched them grow up and do the same as we had done. I would have grown old with my sweetheart and been buried next to him. It would have been that simple.

Now I would watch as Aria flirted with the countless number of strange men. I was in love with a man I barely knew and he loved me back. In a town like this nothing would be either simple or normal. I wouldn't know what to do with anything that came my way. Here I had to take it day-by-day, hour-by-hour. It was excruciatingly boring. I had always enjoyed planning my perfect future. Now I wasn't even sure if I had a future at all.

I crawled out of my cold bubble of thoughts and my warm bath. I went to try to get some rest in the last few hours before sunrise, but before I could make it to my bed I saw a shadow under the doorway. I froze, instantly becoming aware of every sound. I breathed as quietly as I could and told my pulse to keep it down a little. I tiptoed quietly to the door and looked through the crack between where the door and wall met. It was too dark in the hallway to even see a silhouette. All I could see was a tall dark blob surrounded by shadows, not enough to make a guess of who it would be. I backed away slowly and crawled into bed, praying that whoever it was would be on their way soon. Although I did not think I would sleep at all after knowing that some strange person was hanging around outside my door, I fell asleep as soon as I blinked and slept dreamlessly.

When I woke I felt as heavy as a rock. Aria was already at the mirror brushing out her brown hair. "Who are you dressing up for?" I asked as she brushed through her already untangled hair over and over again. I got up and grabbed my own comb.

"Maybe I would just like to look really nice for today. It is a holiday," she made her excuse. I rolled my eyes heavily at her. "Oh all right, perhaps a few boys caught my attention last night. Perhaps I want to look a little nicer for them." She stuck pins in her hair to keep it out of her face. "Look who's talking!" she stared at me as I twisted my hair into a bun Mother had taught me. "Why are *you* getting all dressed up?"

"At least I have *one* man on my mind instead of a few. Plus, as you said, why can't someone just look really nice for a holiday?" I used her own words against her and she huffed at being caught. "If it makes you feel any better, you have met him."

She raised her eyebrows. "Really, is that a fact?" she asked sarcastically.

"Yes, it is. You know that tall blonde angel with the eyes and the body to die for? Is it ringing any bells yet, Aria?"

"No," she teased, "I can't recall anyone that might fit that description. Oh, you mean that kitchen boy with the slight personality defect!" she laughed. I poked her with a pin. "So, Harro? You really like him don't you?"

"Yes, and he really likes me. I think you're just jealous because I may be getting into a serious relationship while you only have those expendable toys to fiddle with."

"You're just jealous that I can fiddle around. You're getting old, Reenie," she laughed, scurrying out of the room with her hair loosely bouncing behind her.

GOOD ADVICE

As I walked out behind her Harro was suddenly at my side. "How was your night?"

"You don't want to know."

"I do," he argued.

"Oh, really?" He nodded. I continued jokingly, "Well, I had an awful dream and woke up in the middle of the night. Then, when I went to fetch water to bathe I was scared to death by a creepy man that had been standing behind me the entire time. When he went up to my room to help with the water he, unashamedly, tried to seduce me back to his room. Not to mention a shadow under my door before I fell asleep again." We came into the main room. "Over all I had a lovely night. How was yours?"

He laughed at my sarcasm. "Well, I woke up when I heard someone pumping water. I watched as a young girl filled her pail and I helped her with it. Once in her room I tried to seduce her right then and there, but she rejected me. I almost convinced her back to my room, but the strange girl was very headstrong. I went to sleep again in a cold bed with no one to comfort me." He laughed again.

"Good morning, Thomas," he nodded to a man coming down from his room.

"'Morning, Harro," the man named Thomas nodded back.

He turned to me, "I must leave you. One of my jobs is to deliver papers once in a while. I'll see you tonight." He bowed and walked off.

"He is so handsome," Aria said from behind me, biting into a waffle.

"Yes, he is," I sighed.

"Not him, you idiot! *Him*," she nodded to a lean young man. He had brown hair and brown eyes and a blinding smile. His laugh was contagious to the friends that surrounded him. "I'd like to know him."

"You'd *like* to know him? Aria, I do believe that you are either losing your touch or he has struck a chord."

"What do you mean? I'm not losing my touch! And I'm only admiring from afar."

"I had once admired Taylor from afar and look how we turned out. A few more months and he would have proposed to me. Oh!" I squealed. "I think my little sister is taking a big step. You're growing up and leaving your toys behind." I clapped my hands excitedly. She only stared at me for a moment and returned her attention to her food. "Well, I suppose he really is cute. He looks like he's well liked . . . strong . . . keen . . . kind. I think he's just what you need." She continually ignored me.

I stepped out into the street; no snow. It was only a little chilly but the sun warmed me through to the bone. I walked slowly down the street. There were people in the market again and men in the bar. This place was so happy it was unreal. It reminded me of one of my dolls when I was young; her ruby red lips had been forcefully painted on her porcelain skin. After all I had put her through I'm sure that, if she could, she would have frowned and grimaced. Maybe that's what this town was doing. It was painting a smile on itself to cover up all the bad things. It was only a façade.

My mind went off to a time when I had acted like that once. I was seven and still wore pigtails to school. William had always been a mean boy to all the little girls, but he and I were enemies. He had tried to take my cookie once, as he had taken Anna's. I wasn't very happy about that so I stamped on his foot. He cried and tried to say that I did it for no reason. That day he had been put in the corner for stealing and lying. I was still upset when I got home but when Mother asked how school was I put on a smile and told her it was just fine. This town was pretending to be just fine even though its history was long and dreary. At least they were trying for each other.

I slipped into the bookstore as Aria and I had done the day before. I looked at the books and chose the same one that had immediately caught my attention the day before: *Maria Lenark*. I sat down with it and carefully laid the old book on the table. I flipped through many heavy, yellowed pages. The writing was old and swirly. As I skimmed the pages I found that no one knew where Maria had come from. She never told anyone much about her past. She came to the little town bearing a child, a boy she would come to name Samuel. At first the people had feared Maria for being such a powerful witch but once her son was born and she showed her compassion she was quickly accepted.

She had an affair with a strange young man on the outskirts of town known only as Old Shia. He would be her three daughters' father. Poor Old Shia had been killed in a bar brawl.

I closed the book. I couldn't take any more news of anyone else dying even if it had been over a hundred years ago. Father died. Mother was killed. Old Shia was killed. Maria was killed. Samuel was killed—too bad he didn't go all the way. There was so much death surrounding me.

I felt something pull at my skirt, pulling me from the dark pool of my mind. It was a little girl with a nearly toothless smile. "Do you want to see some magic?" she whispered eagerly. I just nodded and smiled back. She surprised me by crawling up on my lap. I put my arm around her waist so as she wouldn't fall.

"Watch this!" she held out her little hand face up and stared at it intently. I watched as her hand grew red and her grin grew wide. Little sparks of fire burst out. I jumped. She chuckled proudly. She cupped her hands, "Look!" I did. What I saw amazed me. There was fresh clear water in her tiny hands. She parted her hands and I was ready for it to drop to her pretty little dress and soak it. As it fell it vanished quickly and completely.

I clapped my hands nervously, "You are very good at that."

"I bet I'm not as good as you are, Miss. I'm not in a big family of witches and I've only just started," she grumbled. "I bet you're really powerful!"

I shook my head, "I'm not even a witch. I don't have any magic."

She frowned and wrinkled her forehead. Her green eyes looked confused as she twirled bits of her blonde hair between her stubby fingers. "But Mommy said Lubelle is your ancestor. She said that you and your sissy would be real powerful."

"I'm sure she must've been talking about someone else."

She shrugged, "I guess so. I'll see you later, Missy!" She crawled down from my lap and scampered out of the little store, skipping along the roads without a care in the world.

I shook my head. Why would these people be spreading outrageous rumors like that? These people were so strange and meddlesome. Now they were infesting their children with ideas that my sister and I were witches. Now that I thought about it everyone kept looking at me as if they expected something wondrous. It was as if they expected me to shoot colorful lights or make day turn to night and have the stars rain down on us, as if I was the new Maria Lenark. They expected something special . . . and I was disappointing them.

No!

They had no right to think I was a witch. They had no right to think that they knew me. I wasn't disappointing them; they were just making up stories to make their lives a little more entertaining. They were only in a mood because I wasn't playing a role in their ridiculous fairytales.

I looked up to see a redheaded librarian peeking at me from behind a book. I snorted impolitely and marched out of the little store. I kept walking past the market and past another bookstore. On the left was a dark shop. I could only make out a few candle glows through the thick dark curtains. No one came or went in the minutes I watched the door. I thought it would be a nice quiet place to rest and think for a moment so I went through the heavy door.

The front room was dark but I could make out a few pictures on the wall. It took me a minute to figure out what they were. They were zodiac symbols. I tried to recall what mother had told me I was, but I couldn't remember. Through a beaded doorway I heard someone. They were wheezing painfully, so I peeked through the beads to see if anyone was hurt.

An old woman was leaned back in a big comfy chair. She was the one wheezing. No wonder; she must have been ancient. Her face was covered in wrinkles and her eyes were sunken in a little. The veins under her dark skin stuck out in her frail hands. Those hands shook and her eyes rolled back to show only the whites. Only then did I notice another woman sitting in front of her. She had just handed the old woman a piece of cloth, a shirt. She looked very worried but did nothing to help the elderly woman. Slowly, the old woman came to. She didn't look weak anymore. She looked strong and brave like a warrior.

"Kari?" the young woman asked. "What's going on? What did you see?"

The old woman, Kari, shook her head over and over again. She handed back the shirt, "I'm sorry my dear. What you feared was correct. Your husband is unfaithful."

The young woman held back tears, "With who was he unfaithful?"

"A woman younger than you, but a lot like you. I think you already know, Wanda." Kari gave Wanda a sad look as the youthful lady burst into tears. "It was your littlest sister." I moved just in time for Wanda to dash out of the shop.

"How may I help you, Renee?" Kari smoothed the sheet that was set over her small round table. "I know you're there. You may enter." I did so shyly, like a child that had been caught trying to steal a snack. "You have nothing to be afraid of, child. My bark is still strong but my bite faded long ago," she chuckled. "Sit, sit."

I sat in the chair opposite from her, wondering how she knew my name. "I'm sorry for watching, Mrs. Kari. I didn't mean to intrude."

"Just call me Kari. Curiosity is not a sin, just be wary. What would you like to know today?"

"What do you mean?" I questioned her. There were a lot of things I wanted to know. How many stars were there in the sky? What is the meaning of life? What is going on with all the legends here? What will happen to Harro and me?

"As you saw, I answer questions. Do you have anything you need answered? And nothing silly like: Why do a strawberry's seeds grow on the outside? I only answer serious questions."

I thought for a moment, "There's a lot I would like to know—"

"Not what you would *like* to know, only what you *need* to know." I stared at Kari. She sighed, "Wanda *needed* to know what her husband was up to. If she didn't, she would have wasted more of her young life on that wretched boy. She would become even more heartbroken. If she fixes the problem now she may be able to spare all of them a lot of pain. She and the boy are still young enough to move on and she may be able to salvage her relationship with her sister. So . . . what do you *need* to know?" she folded her hands in front of her.

I thought about it for a long time. Kari didn't seem to mind the wait. As I thought, I could start to smell the fragrance of her candles. They smelled like a cross between French vanilla and honeysuckles. Their scent sparked a thought in my mind. I told her sadly, "I need to know what's going to happen to Aria and me."

She nodded knowingly, "That, my dear, is a very wise question; a very important question in your situation." How did she know my situation? How did she know about my sister? "I must assume that you have heard people whispering your names and I won't bother to tell you the meaning of it all. It's not in my place to tell you. However, it is my place to answer your question. Give me your hands." She held out hers and I put mine in them. I was never one to believe in fortune telling but I was always one to try everything possible. Her pupils dilated. She started breathing hard, harder than she had with Wanda. Her wheezing came and didn't stop as her eyes rolled back into her head. She clutched my hands until they seared with pain, but I did not take them back. She trembled with her visions. Suddenly she let go and threw my hands away.

She rubbed her hands and I rubbed mine. "Forgive me," she said. "Oh, my dear child, oh, oh, oh . . ."

"What? What's wrong?" I pleaded. I had to know what she had seen. I believed now. I would believe anything that old woman told me as long as I had something to look forward to . . . or try to avoid. I would believe that I would walk upside down tomorrow, that I would turn into a rabbit, even that my parents would come back from the dead, as long as she told me.

"My dear, your journey will be harsh and quick. You have little time left," she whispered to me. "Take heed of my advice! Listen to your sister. Be wary of those near you. Listen to your head and to your heart, child. Maria will help you on your way. This is all I was meant to do for you." I stumbled from her room and into the next as she spoke. With my hand on the doorknob she called, "One more thing, child. Hear me! Beware of Samuel's son!" I sprinted out of her shack and down the street with people giving me strange glances. I rounded a corner into an empty alley.

We were going to die! We were going to suffer. I would try doing as the woman said; maybe her advice would save us. Maybe I could change our fate. I would listen to Aria more carefully now, I would try to believe her. I would be more careful of who I trusted. I would listen to myself, whatever that meant. Most of all I would be on the lookout for Samuel's son, whoever he was.

Oh! I just wanted to do exactly the opposite. I wanted to be a normal nineteen-year-old girl. I wanted to completely and totally ignore every word my sister said. I shouldn't have to be careful of whom I trusted or what I did. It should be safe. I didn't want to have to listen to my head or listen to my heart. I wanted to be spontaneous and free. And I did not want to look out for a dead spirit's evil son that may or may not be the death of me. My head hurt from all the turmoil and my heart ached with it. All I ever wanted was some excitement in my old life and now I would give anything just to go back to it. I wanted to be normal. I wanted to be safe. I wanted to be happy.

I wanted to be home.

Parades of Fate and Confusion

I cried there in my hiding place for a while. Eventually I dried my eyes and walked out into the street. I had to find Aria and tell her what Kari had told me. I needed to tell her. I couldn't bare it on my own and it was going to be her funeral, too.

I walked slowly down the streets, passing people who whispered and glanced and murmured. I ignored all of it. I was numb to it all and couldn't care anymore. I just kept thinking of more and more horrific ways to die. There was drowning, freezing, burning, stabbing, poisoning, falling, strangling, and more. Worse yet, there were and endless number of combinations. Even worse, possibly the worst of all, these options of death were upon Aria as well. She was only fourteen. She was so young, so innocent. I couldn't let her die. I wouldn't let her die. I made an oath to myself, walking on those busy streets full of unknowing people. I promised myself that if Aria died, I would follow quickly.

When I swung the inn door open I spotted Aria flirting with yet another boy, not the cute one she had pointed out the previous night. She saw me and there must have been a look on my face or a way about me that she stopped dead in the middle of her conversation and ran after me to our room. She shut the door behind her and locked it. "What's going on? What happened? Are you okay?" she fretted.

"I'm fine . . . for now," I told her. "Aria, I went to a fortune teller and, I know this sounds crazy coming from me, but I believed her." My sister raised her brows until they were hidden in her hair. "Aria, you need to sit down. I need to tell you what she told me."

She sat down beside me in a sober mood. "Tell me everything." So I did. I told her about the stares we had been getting from the people. She had noticed as well. I told her about what I'd read in Maria's book in the library. I told her about the little girl and what she had said. I had to repeat that part because Aria had thought she'd misunderstood me or misheard me. Her eyes got huge when I told her again and the words came out clearly.

I continued on to what I'd seen at Kari's fortune telling shack. I told her about what she told me. The only part I left out was when I stopped and had an emotional breakdown. I only said that I came straight to tell her.

"This can't be right. Why would we have to be so careful in this little town? We can't truly be witches. I've never even pulled a rabbit out of a hat. These people must have us confused with someone else," Aria tried desperately to reason.

"Then how would you explain Kari?"

"She's old and weird. She could just be messing with you."

"No, Aria," I told her. "This was very, very real. Not even an old crackpot like her could come up with this stuff. Aria, I don't know what to do. I'm scared," I admitted.

"Neither do I, sister," she sighed heavily, "And all we've got to go on is a bunch of stupid riddles!"

I thought for a while. We had to figure out why everyone thought we were witches. We had to figure out who Samuel's son is. We had to figure out how to avoid our inevitable deaths until we could figure everything out. "Perhaps we could figure some things out during the parade. It is tonight."

"Yes, it is," Aria told me with no confidence in her weary voice.

"I'm going to go down to the main room for a while before it begins." I headed to the door. "Are you coming?"

"I'm going to stay up here for a while, go ahead," she waved me on. I shrugged and went down. I sat down at the bar, "Hello, Barbara." I smiled at her and ordered some pasta that didn't sound too different from the ones we had in Mar.

I looked around the room at all of the people. I quickly found the boy Aria had been admiring the night before. Turns out, all you had to do to find him was look for the crowd that was having the best time and there he would be, a light shining its rays on whoever desired it. I watched as he arm-wrestled with another young man. They both grunted and their faces turned red. The veins on his huge arm throbbed out. I guess he wasn't as lanky as he looked. They finally gave up, being too much of a match for the other, not having moved an inch.

"Are you excited?" Barbara asked as she set down a plate of pasta. "I know I am."

"Yes, very much so," I smiled and took a bite. It was delicious as everything else here seemed to be. "What all happens during the parade?"

"Well," she looked around to make sure her mother, Chene, wasn't listening, "You know mother doesn't like anyone saying anything, but I'll tell you. First, we purify the streets and go to Maria's home. Then we all gather into the streets to have fun. There's food and dancing and Kari will be there—she tells people's fortunes." Little did Barbara know I'd already had the *pleasure* of meeting Kari. Barbara glanced to the kitchen door where her mother was coming out of, "I'll see you later." She hurried off to more work. I saw Aria's young hopeful follow her, tying an apron around his waist. He must be the one who helps cook all of this glorious food and it was a good thing. If anything did become of the two of them there would be little tasteful food in the house if Aria was completely in charge of the cooking.

As soon as I realized that Barbara wasn't going to be able to speak with me again I started thinking of all the questions I could have asked her. Too late now. I ate my food and watched the sky dim as it grew closer to the twilight and to the start of the parade. I was sad to see the blue fade to pinks and purples, into gold and reds and disappear into another gray-blue.

Harro sat down beside me as comfortably as a cat would, "Good evening."

"Good evening," I said.

"What's wrong?" he questioned as he twirled with a loose bit of lace on my sleeve.

I shook my head, "I've just got a lot on my mind." I changed the subject quickly, knowing that he was about to ask what exactly was on my mind. "Shouldn't you be doing chores?" The sun finally set and one by one people retreated outside.

"No, the parade is about to start so I got out of jail duty a little early," he said sarcastically. The noise grew outside as more people assembled. He stood up and suggested, "Would you like me to accompany you? I wouldn't want you to get lost on a night like this." He smiled at me mischievously, tempting me to have a little fun. I took his arm and he led me into the streets.

WALKS AND REVELATIONS

Men and women were dropping flower petals of all colors along the cobblestones, not a single one of them from a red rose. The trail went on and on to the outskirts of town like an entrance to a grand wedding. Harro whispered in my ear, "It's tradition to purify the way to Maria's home before the march. Only pure souls should be able to walk with us. That means that Samuel *shouldn't* be there." I gripped his arm excitedly when the people in the parade entered my sight, but in the back of my mind what he said nagged at me. Just the way he said it had me worried.

Adults in colored robes led the way gripping white candles and deep in the middle children formed a white mass. "When they recite their poem, be very quiet as not to disturb anyone," Harro told me. I looked at him curiously for an answer but the townspeople had started to hum. When my escort squeezed my hand I joined in, feeling my chest vibrate. The people of the march started to speak. It sounded as if they were reciting an oath rather than a poem but some strange flow of rhythm and sweetness flowed behind their words.

Oh, black magic, depart from us, leave us lighthearted
Free Maria's soul of her old use of you
White magic cleanse us, enter our souls
And let dear Maria come among us

They continued down the street. Harro pulled me along with the following crowd. My hands were sweaty and my heart thrummed in my ears as fast as a hummingbird's wings. I was excited . . . and utterly terrified. I had been raised to not believe in silly things such as this but the thought of seeing Maria's spirit among these living souls alerted a part of me that I didn't know I had. If Maria was real what was stopping Samuel from coming? I swept away my thoughts and trusted my guardian. He strode tall and proud beside me unknowing of my fears as the others carried on.

Good you were to him with a guiding light
With anger in his heart he struck you down
To stain your Eden with red, red blood and grow of it forevermore
When he stayed you stayed keeping peace between our worlds
For this we honor you brave Maria and in thanks for our gifts

I could see Maria's old house now as we crowded around it. Harro stood me only a little ways from the turmoil of a garden. It felt like he was testing me. How close can Renee get to the spook house without freaking out?

We release you, Samuel, from this place
And free you kind Maria from you duties
We ask for blessings and paths of light for our New
For in this night, Maria, we honor

Their speech and our humming stopped as the last person settled into place around Maria's old home. It was old and falling apart and the flowers were left to run amuck. Shutters and doors were falling away. Windowpanes were shattered, the roof bore a thousand holes, and the stone chimney lay half crumbled on the roof, the rest scattered across the ground. Beyond the house was a black abyss of pastures and fields. The mountains stuck into the sky like spears and somewhere in the distance a wolf called to his pack.

Somehow, despite the gruesome state of the old house, it held an ancient beauty. This very house had raised Maria and her son, Samuel, and her daughters, who passed on the witchery. This house had seen quite a bit; I wished I could sit there for days and listen to its great stories. The house deteriorated with pride and dignity the way a knight rode into battle to meet his death. It deserved a rest from the pressure surrounding it, all the magic weaving through it. It was devastatingly beautiful.

When I finally allowed my eyes to rest on the blood fed garden of red roses I became completely terrified. I clutched at Harro's arm. The roses were spelled from Death itself and dripped of it in every moment. The roses were the color of blood. Not the blood that came from a paper cut on your finger when reading a book, but of the blood spilt in war straight from a soldier's heart. It was from the heart of a brave soul that unwillingly shed its tear dropped rubies. It was the blood of Maria's living, breathing . . . dying body as it lay at her only son's feet. The wicked petals looked leathery and cracked like the binding of an ancient book or the wings of a dead bat. Where bright green leaves and stem were supposed to sprout, there was blackness. These parts were the black of burnt flesh and seemed to reach to you as if trying to draw on blood from your veins. The thorns were a sickly brown, curved and twisted to a lethal point ready for a drink of innocent blood as soon as it could prick.

As the glassy moon reached its peak in the sky the crowd bowed their heads and all whispered their own prayers and forgiveness. I bowed my head as well and listened to the words of others: "Leave here Samuel, your time here has passed." "Thank you Maria." "Oh God protect us from the anger of these lost souls. Spare us." Though Harro stood at my side I could not decipher his words. He mumbled them in such a deep, quiet voice I found I was not meant to hear his prayer.

Off in the crowd I saw a man, head barely bent and not uttering a single word. He was looking around, eyes darting every which way as if he was observing us. He caught my eye and I looked down immediately.

We lifted our heads and, one-by-one, departed from the lonely house, falling back to the bright town to celebrate. As I looked around again the man was nowhere to be seen.

Harro walked me slowly to the bright lights as if to make a distinction between the darkness and the light. Children skipped along throwing sparks from their hands and making coins disappear. They laughed and giggled and I hoped Aria had woken up for this. She would just love for a young man to give her a flower formed from thin air. At that I thought of Harro. He was only a little older than I was. He was smart and courteous. Not to mention that he was drop dead gorgeous and that any of my friends back home would fight over him the moment they let lay eyes on him. I came to find that I was starting to like him more than I thought I could; perhaps more than I thought I should. I was attracted to his muscled body, to his voice and to his very presence.

Ahead I saw the celebrating people talking in groups or eating their strange food. Musicians played for the couples that swirled about and the children that bounced up and down. We were nearing them and I was expecting Harro to lead me to a food table but instead he took me by the hand and my waist and led me into the movement of people. If I wouldn't have been so terrified I would've thrown my head back with laughter and smiled widely with him. Instead I sloppily followed him, "I don't know this dance!" I had to shout over the people and music for him to hear me.

"You don't have to!" he shouted back. The hand on my waist got heavier and the hand holding mine grew tighter. "Just follow my lead!" we bounced and swirled along with the others and I found a rhythm to the movements. Out of the corner of my eye I saw Aria flirting shamelessly with a poor boy . . . *again.* He didn't look like he minded much at all. I laughed and smiled at her, happy to see her out of her earlier stupor. She had a twinkle in her eyes that I had never seen before. I looked back at my partner. He had a dangerous look on his face. It was the face of a snake right before it struck; the face of the hunter as it lured in its prey. It was the face of a man with an evil mission. But before I could even be sure I saw it he was smiling again. He twirled me out of the crowd to a table of food. He started picking freely and I followed his lead. When he offered me an apple I couldn't help but think of the fairytale Mother once told me of the woman who ate an apple that caused her death. Though I knew it was silly, even in this world of magic, I turned it down.

"Reenie!" Aria ran up to me, tailed by a short boy with choppy brown hair and a crooked smile. I recognized him as the boy from the kitchen. The same boy that had been arm wrestling. "Reenie, this is Luke. Luke this is my sister, Renee." She introduced us.

"It's nice to meet you," he bowed breathlessly; Aria had forced him to dance with her, if you could call it forcing. I nodded to him. He swallowed nervously, "Hello, Harro." He did not bow to him.

Harro smiled smugly at a joke I wasn't part of, "Hello, Luke. Enjoying the celebrations? It's a lovely night." Luke only nodded and walked away with Aria following worriedly. I'd never seen two men act so strangely to one another in all my life.

I turned to Harro, "What was that all about?" He just went back to eating without bothering to answer me. I turned on my heel muttering, "Stupid rude boys! Absolutely unbelievable! Outrageous!" I turned around a corner of a tent only to see him there. I jumped knowing there's no possible way he had slipped in front of me. "You people and your silly magic!" I began to walk away but he grabbed my arm. I looked at him accusingly. I tried to yank my arm away but his grip tightened and he pulled me to him fiercely. He was angry that I had walked away from him; I could feel the vibes rolling off of his tense body. When he spoke he did so quietly and gently, "I apologize for being rude." The words only seemed to be filled with more threat when spoken in his tone. "It is only a town rumor that doesn't need to worry your pretty little head. I just get tired of hearing it." His grasp on my arm didn't loosen a bit and it was starting to throb. "Now, if you don't mind, please, don't ever walk away from me again." He stared at my face waiting for an answer. Only a husband, or perhaps a slave owner, would talk to a lady like that.

I swallowed my fear and pulled out the courage my father had passed down to me. "I will do what I wish. No man owns me, especially not you." I returned his stare. "Now, *I'm not asking*. Let go of me." When he did I rubbed my sore arm. "You have such a way with the ladies, Harro." I narrowed my eyes at him for a second and started on my way to the inn. I felt Harro grab my arm again and I turned quickly to slap him. My hand left a large red print on his cheek. Seeing that red mark satisfied a part of me so much that I wanted to laugh in his beautiful face. This time when I walked away he did not follow.

I walked through happy crowds to the inn. I must've been one of the only ones—or *the* only one—to be angry. I had no smile on my face as I walked by Aria and her cute new toy, Luke. I saw her eye me questioningly and shook my head. Not taking the hint she grabbed Luke's hand and raced after me. I sat in front of the fire in the still empty room and stared at the flames. I was finally starting to relax when Aria came through the door to sit beside me, and motioned for Luke to do the same. I knew she was observing my face to see where to start but it was her dear Luke who spoke first.

"What did he do? Did he hurt you?" he asked knowing I would know what he was talking about.

"Who?" Aria eyed him curiously.

"Harro," I explained. I looked at Luke, "He was quite rude after you left." I told him what happened. His face only grew grimmer, not surprised. "Luke, I need to know what that supposed rumor is."

He nodded and sighed, "It's more like a legend than a rumor. I don't want to be the reason for you two to not see each other—I mean it could all just be suspicion—but . . . you still need to know. Nice women like the two of you deserve much better." He ran his long fingers through his hair and began, "It was said that Samuel had a son. It was said that Samuel had put a spell on a woman so she would love him. She was one of the most beautiful in the city at the time. She had long wavy blond hair with blue eyes like ice. She carried herself as if she deserved to be royalty. It was that selfishness that had drawn Samuel to her. They were both greedy and arrogant. That woman soon bore his child. As soon as he found out he cast her away as useless and denied that he was the child's father. He was very young then and still had enough common sense to keep that mayhem from his mother, Maria. The woman had her child. He had her blond hair and blue eyes, but would most likely have his father's build and wickedness. Some say that Samuel killed the boy and his ex-lover. If so that would mean all of Maria's line were good, coming from her three daughters, Tabitha, Eurose, and Lubelle. It is known that I am a descendent of Tabitha.

"Others say that Samuel left his discarded family to fend on their own and that his son grew to be strong and powerful. Some say that he was powerful enough that he drank a potion to keep him young forever. Samuel's heir had no soul to trade with so he gave up his chance to have an heir of his own. Harro moved here a year or two ago. I believe, along with many others, that he had just moved *back.*" I gasped and he shook his head. "Yes. Harro is the immortal heir of Samuel. With me being the heir of Tabitha you can see how that can cause some," he searched for a word, "difficulties."

"That's horrible! Doesn't that mean that he's powerful enough to enslave all the witches in the city?" I was outraged. How could sweet—however temperamental—Harro be evil and ready to bring about this town's Doomsday? Yet some part of me knew this was true. Some deep part of my soul and mind told me to be cautious around him. He was dangerous.

"Yes, it's legend that he will bring about destruction. There is one forgotten myth that is starting to come forth again in hope of a savior. One of Lubelle's line is said to come from out of nowhere and defeat Samuel's heir, drive away Samuel himself, and set Maria Lenark free. The town seems to think this hero is one of you." He put his hand up to stop us from interrupting, but it did no good.

"Us? We're just girls. We can't defeat evil spirits and things like that! We're just from Mar!" Aria went on. She paused for my usual continuance of her complaints.

I just stared. When I finally found my tongue my words were blunt, "Are you crazy?!" They both jumped back, surprised by my aggressiveness. "I know Aria already told you about our mother. Why would you think we could be—or even want to be—witches? Why would we save more witches? What is *wrong* with you people?"

"Look I know it does sound crazy. It's probably not even true, but haven't you learned anything about us? We're not black magic users," Luke stayed calm. "Look around and look at all the witches. If you were one of us wouldn't you hold on to any hope, any chance at all, that all of the darkness would go away? Wouldn't you wish that you didn't have to keep your children in on nights of the new moon and put out cups of water and watch your children grow up in this one place? We don't have anywhere to go! We can't even go on the other side of the island! If we leave this place and they find out about what we are we will meet the same fate as your mother. Renee, you and Aria may be our only hope if it really is you." We were all quiet and Aria had her head dipped low. There was too much false pressure on her shoulders. I could feel tears stinging my eyes.

I took a deep breath, "I'm sorry, Luke. I hope your people find the right person soon." I stood up and walked to the stairs.

I heard Luke's last words to me, "Look around you, Renee. *Look* and try to *see*."

SEEING IS BELIEVING

I went up to my room and stared out the window. I could see, thank you very much. I wasn't blind. Looking meant seeing. So I looked down on the streets. Elderly people watched their grandchildren and spent the night with their loved ones, not knowing which second would be the last. Mothers and fathers watched their children at play and tried to teach them. Older children enjoyed life to the fullest and smiled and laughed until they cried. They found love among others and of course the pain as well. Young children giggled at their powers and played with their friends . . . they were so young and innocent. They didn't know what was going to happen to them; they didn't care. They were also witches. They would learn spells, hexes, vexes, and potions. They would have to choose between white magic and black magic. They were witches. They were children.

That's what Luke had meant. I'd seen the kids. I'd seen the people. I'd seen their joy and love and passion. I'd shared some of it. But I'd never noticed how very fragile their lives were. The only reason the outside world didn't burn them all is because they were either scared or they didn't know of this town's whereabouts. They were trapped here. Few would be able to travel across other lands and explore the world. Few would meet new people and find a place of their own. Even worse, is knowing that even fewer would survive. Mother died. Yes, she died because of what she was thought to be—now, what she might've been. Her life had been like a crystal vase; beautiful and happy and raising tulips . . . and ever so breakable. One loose hand, one slip, one moment of lost attention and the vase would fall and shatter into a million pieces, never to be mended. Those shards hurt my heart like when you try to sweep them under the rug and step on them later. These people never chose their powers or ancestors. They didn't have a say in anything except what to make out of what they've been given. These weren't witches and magic users. These were people, just people.

Tears of shame had bathed my face and I went to wash it. I looked at the mirror. It was smooth and clean. I splashed water on my face and when I looked again there were two reflections. One was of a pale puffy-eyed girl with brown lox and brown eyes: a poor, self-pitying me. The other was of a small woman. Her skin was dark and of mixed races. Her hair was dark and twisted about her head. Her eyes were dark and strong and her mouth was set in a line. Her face was completely unreadable of any emotion. When I had taken it all in, I realized that this girl was Maria Lenark. I turned quickly to look behind me but there was only empty space to be seen. I looked back at the mirror and there she was smiling at her own joke. "Maria?" I asked. She looked around and put a finger over her lips. I stayed quiet. She pointed down to the water in the marble bowl. I looked back at her. Her eyes were in earnest and she nodded her head furiously. She pointed again I looked into the water. I saw it ripple then waves formed in it and I found that I couldn't look away. Suddenly, Samuel's face appeared in the liquid. His scream was silent and as the water tamed his face deteriorated. I looked at Maria who shook her head solemnly and turned. I looked behind me, still expecting to see her walking away. Of course she wasn't there, nor was she to be found in the mirror when I looked back.

What did her little trick mean? Does water hurt witches? Of course not, they drink water, just as I do. Samuel's face . . . it was wretched. His face was sallow and pale before he disappeared. His hair was a black tangled mess. His eyes were as black as a dark icy ocean in the depth of a winter night. His teeth were yellow as he screamed. As the water had settled, his face grew to be the single most terrifying thing I'd ever seen. Those corn-like teeth broke and fell apart. His lips wrinkled and shrank. His hair turned to dust and his black eyes sunk in and inked out. His frosty skin fizzled and bubbled away. But what did it mean? Did water hurt him? That had to be it! Good witches must be burnt with fire and evil ones die in water. Water was good and fire was bad. Everything was falling in place. There was only one problem: I wasn't a witch. Neither was Aria.

I looked back at the pool of water, angry and frustrated. I hated the people for killing Mother, I hated Harro for what he might do, I hated myself for being so rude to Luke, I hated this world for being so cruel and violent—I was just soaked. I opened my eyes when I felt water splash onto my face and arms and dress. The water had flown right out of the sink. I looked in the mirror for Maria thinking that maybe she was trying to get my attention. She wasn't there. Aria wasn't anywhere to be seen, waiting to splash more water on me. There was no other explanation than that I had done it. Without touching the water or blowing on it *I* had done this. So it was true! I was a witch! I was magic!

No, no, no! This couldn't be! That meant my mother was a witch! They were all right. It was our destiny to come here from "nowhere". We were it. Maria stood in the mirror nodding and smiling and fading again. I didn't want to be a witch. I didn't want to be a hero. I never asked for any of this but here I was, picking up more cards in this game and being forced into the move they wanted with no way to fold.

I dried off quickly and ran down the stairs. Aria was hunched over a table staring at a candle. Luke had gone out again, leaving the room silent. I stood there not saying a word. She went on staring, blinking away tears with no knowledge of my being there. The candle went out then flickered back to life. More tears spilt from her eyes. She grabbed the burning wick. It should have caused pain but she slowly drew her unscarred hand back. "What does this mean?" she whimpered to herself.

"I don't know," I said. She startled and stared at my wet dress. "We're witches aren't we?" I sighed and answered my own question, "We are. Aria, Luke was right . . . and I'm frightened."

"You saw Maria Lenark, too?" she asked. I nodded and told her what happened. "Wow. She kind of just formed out of the fire for me. She pointed to a glass of water and I saw Samuel screaming and fizzing away. I think you're right. He can be hurt by water. Then, the flame started to look less and less like Maria and more like plain fire. I was so nervous I just reached in for her. I took my hand out but wasn't hurt and, well, you saw the rest." We stared at the fire hoping to see Maria and maybe get some answers. "I don't want this," she said. "I don't want to be a witch or be a hero. I just want to be a normal fourteen year old. I want to have a protective father and a worrisome mother. I want to flirt with normal boys and have you tell me how vain I am, just like normal."

"I didn't ask for any of it either. I just want to hear Father tell me I should act more like a lady. I want to be able to cook with Mother. As weird as it sounds, I want to have to make sure you don't skip school and I want a normal guy to actually like me. I want to think that all of this is just a dream, but I know it's not. Dreams don't hurt this bad," I said. I was tired of being tired. I was tired of being hurt.

"Father will never tell us to clean and Mother will never teach us her recipes. Everything's been turned upside down. I just want to go home," she said quietly and hopelessly as we walked up to the room. We slept soundly that night, having cried out all of our energy. It was like that first night we slept on that Godforsaken boat. We had been so stressed after our parents' death, running, hiding, and everything else that when we finally slept we didn't care if we ever woke up or not. We had woken up, though, and we had been brought here. It had to be for a reason and we had to do the best with the cards we had. For now we lay our cards face down and took a break from the game. I could feel myself slip into the dark warmness of sleep and I was as thankful as I had ever been.

When I did wake up the moon was beginning to set and the sun was not yet up. I heard footsteps outside our door and I knew I needed to get up and lock it, but as soon as I saw Maria guarding the door and protecting me from any evil that might lie on the other side I drifted off again. When I woke up to stay awake Aria was washing up. I found that the door was locked and so was the window. Maria sure wasn't going to let anything happen to the saviors. I changed and headed down to the kitchen with Aria, ready for more answers.

I guess we had expected the happy crowd we had seen yesterday. They should've been smiling and working off hangovers. They should've been telling stories about last night and laughing. Instead, we got the opposite. The people were suddenly sobered and many had puffy, red faces. Some were completely out of it, trying to drink away their pain. Even the children that had been skipping and playing now sat in their parents laps or sat comforting family and friends. I recognized the man from the night before sitting at a table with a young woman. They did not seem frightfully upset. Only their brows were furrowed and lips set in thin lines.

The man was rugged, maybe in his forties. His red hair was buzzed, a puff of red on his chin, and a clean mustache above his lips made him look almost professional. But his cheeks were covered in stubble and his hands were scared. He kept his icy eyes on his beer.

The woman was younger, petite with black hair and cold eyes. She seemed like a soldier . . . or a statue.

I noticed then that there was no speaking in the inn. Even joyful Barbara was in a gloomy mood. She absently took orders and cleaned the tables. We went up to her. "Barbara?" I touched her hand. She drew back and shook her head as she moved away from us. A sad Chene beckoned us into an empty room.

We followed her and asked, "What's happened? What's wrong, Chene?" She sat on the fresh sheets of the bed after closing the door and bowed her head tiredly. "Girls, yesterday you saw how sweet this town can be, didn't you?" We both nodded without a word. "This morning you will hear of how hideous and cruel some people can be. Some souls—one in specific—that rest here and live here are of dark magic and have a heart of coal. On the outside they are stronger than anyone else is but on the inside they are like black dust, easy to chip away. Remember that; remember that you are what you have on the inside and that makes them nothing. Also remember that even the purest can fall if they cannot be strong enough on the outside." Tears rimmed her eyes.

"Chene, I don't understand. Why are you telling us this?" Aria whispered, not breaking the intensity of the moment.

FEELING DEATH

———————— ◉ ————————

"Luke is dead," she said simply and nodded when we gasped. "Last night he was killed. Murdered. His body is being washed and dressed for his funeral. He was found with his eyes scorched and his hands boiled by water. A white-hot stake had been buried deep in his chest. Whoever killed him knew to use fire. He must have seen terrible things for his eyes to be like that, scorched by evil. It's time, girls. We will either parish soon or survive to see times of harsh recovery."

"Chene, you're speaking in riddles!"

"Samuel's heir is acting! You know of whom I speak of. Now that his heir is strong enough Samuel is drawing on his power to be able to hurt the living. For telling you two about Harro, Luke unknowingly gave up his life. Don't let him have died in vain." Chene opened the door and walked away to continue with her weary work saying, "Don't you dare."

We stood paralyzed. Our minds were unable to comprehend what she wished for us to do so when Harro walked in we took no notice that he was the enemy. "I know you heard the tragic news. You both need to rest." He sat me on the edge of the bed and led the frozen Aria back to our room. She must have really liked him to react this badly. I'd never seen her act like this, even when mother died. Luke's loss was different, she was possibly losing—had lost—her other half. Harro returned to the room and closed the door behind him. He sat beside me and rubbed my arm, "It's okay. You'll be okay." He held me in his arms resting his chin on my shoulder. "It's okay."

I knew it wasn't okay. I knew that Luke would never be coming back. I knew that Aria's heart would always secretly burn from now on. I knew that since the night my father died that nothing was even remotely close to okay.

Of course Harro could not hear the thoughts in my head and I could not yet express them. His breath was warm on my neck. It made my hair stand on end and my stomach knot. He kissed my jaw, "Shh." I wasn't sure if he was soothing me or if he was telling me not to scream or move. My brain was slowly realizing that I wasn't safe around him but I still could not make my body move. It was like when that snake bit little Timothy and he couldn't move his foot for a week no matter how hard he tried. Harro kissed my shoulder gently as his fingers twined in the bow of my dress.

I stood up and moved away from him, relieved that my brain had thawed out so quickly and I could think rationally again. I remembered what my mother had once told me, "Listen to me child, though God knows you never do, listen to me this once. Knowledge is power so never tell anyone what you know. The more knowledge you have the bigger a weapon you have." I remembered this now. It wasn't as if I could jump up and run from Harro screaming at him not to touch me. It's not as if I could tell him I know everything and that I know he killed Luke and that my sister and I would defeat him. He would kill me where I stood then finish Aria. I knew he would take no chances at losing his ancient blood feud over two defenseless girls. So I just stood up and said, "I told you last night that you are no gentleman." I opened the door and walked up to Aria, thankful that there were too many witnesses for him to draw me back or strike me. I had just scared myself nearly to death and had to wait outside the door to calm myself. As soon as I walked through the door Aria grabbed my hand and led me back down the hall, down the stairs, and out to the street. "Where are we going?"

"We're going to find someone to help us figure out what we're going to do," she walked swiftly to the bookshop. People looked at us curiously. There we were, two girls that just came to town nearly running for the bookshop that held all the magic of their people after we had denied over and over again that we had anything to do with magic. Some looked at us as if we had gone mad. Some just looked curiously and went on their way. Others eyed us with hope that the determination on our face meant that we would save them. Those people soon started to whisper to their friends and them to others. Some took off to tell their families.

We ignored it all and walked through the wooden door. We started searching the books' titles franticly. The redheaded librarian's eyes grew wide as I found Maria's book and started skimming through it. She shoed everyone out of the library, "Out, out, out! I am closing! Out, all of you!" she closed the door behind them and turned to us. "Who are you?"

I never took my eyes off of Maria's book as I answered her, "I am Renee Thomas and this is my sister, Aria Thomas."

"What do you want?" she asked nervously as she approached us. "What are you here for?"

"According to your people," Aria answered, "we are here to save you." She put up the book she was flipping through and grabbed another. "Who are *you* and what do *you* want?"

"I'm Phyllis and if what you say is true I want to help. Can you prove that your Maria Lenark's descendent?" She eyed us challengingly.

"Not exactly. Until last night we had no idea that we were witches or what was going on or even who Maria was—"

"I can help with that!" she snatched the old book from my hands and flipped to and old family tree. "Are any of these people your family?"

Before Aria even answered Phyllis she asked, "Why does this line end here?" She pointed to a name with an arrow pointing to a blank space to where the heirs would be.

"Well, one woman and her husband left and started a life in some other place, but we know she had a family because she was with child when she left. Well, actually my grandparents know; she left back in their time."

"Oh, my! Aria, look at those names!" I pointed to the pair of names written in fancy script. "Those are Grandfather and Grandmother's names! See, Abigail and Warren Tanner. Do you know what they might have named their daughter?"

Phyllis thought for a moment. "Granny always said that Mrs. Abigail favored the name Sarah. Is that you mother's name? What's your father's name?"

"Yes, her name was Sarah . . . and his name was Joseph," I sat down. I watched Phyllis fill in the empty holes with Sarah and Joseph Thomas then write our names. "You said you could help us, so do just that. Help us."

She nodded and motioned for us to follow her. We followed her through a small hallway to a closet where she pulled away the rug and opened a door in the floor. We followed her down steep stone steps and, for all we cared, to the end of the world and to our deaths. All we had was this one small light of hope and I was willing to cling onto it no matter what. Ahead I saw a candle lit room and heard voices within.

"It has to be them."

"They are only children!"

"It was said that we would be saved in our youth."

"Plus, they came from nowhere."

"They didn't even know that this place existed."

"They didn't even know Maria existed!"

"Nevertheless they are our heroes and we will help them."

"Yes, we will," Phyllis stood up for us when we entered the room. "It truly is them! They are daughters of Sarah, daughter of Abigail and Warren. They are heirs of Lubelle and have newly discovered their powers and, if I'm right in my assumption, they've been visited by Maria." The six elders in the dimly lit room turned to us and we nodded. "Sit and be of use, otherwise, leave." Phyllis's sweet face grew hard and stern at the elders. She ushered us into old chairs as her and the others sat in their own in front of us.

"Start at the beginning, young one," a fat old man with a husky voice waved us on. So we told him our story. We told him of the accusations against mother and explained that where we came from, being a witch meant the death penalty. We told them how Father was so healthy and how he died cold in his bed one night. We told of how we watched Mother be dragged by her long gorgeous hair to her death. We told about how we had to watch and listen to our mother die and how we were forced to run for our lives, leaving everything we knew behind us. They asked about our boat over here and how we jumped ship. They wanted to be caught up until we came into the library and met Phyllis.

So we told them.

We told them everything, taking turns when our paths had separated or one of us had left something out. We went on and on reliving our torments and nightmares so vividly I trembled and Aria nearly left. The elders took all of it in with unreadable, emotionless faces. Phyllis's face was the only one that held emotion, but that was almost worse than none at all. She was pitying us and feeling sorry for us and I was tired of it. At last when we were through with our tale the elders sat there for longer, comprehending and trying to see it in our perspective along with theirs.

They debated in whispers for a long time as we sat there uncomfortably. I couldn't sit still so I paced. I was growing impatient with these old fools. We just needed to be taught how to use our magic and how to use them against Samuel and Harro. Then, we could leave and we could start anew. Again.

They turned to us. "It seems that you young ladies are in fact meant to defeat the evil within this old town and set free Maria's soul so she can finally rest." The old man spoke slowly as he said what everyone already knew when we had first walked into the room. "We shall teach you and guide you."

"Sit," motioned a small old woman. Despite her frailty she looked strong and courageous. She put two candles in front of us on a rickety old table. "Make them go out," she ordered. Aria's went out quickly and flickered back to life. It took me great concentration just to get mine to go out, much less to relight it. "Take your time. Center yourself and concentrate."

I did so as I thought only of the flame and what I wanted it to do. The wick burst into flame once again. Next Phyllis placed bowls of water in front of us. The old woman said, "Make it move—without touching it!"

My water started to ripple and wave and form into a whirlpool. Aria stared intently at her water. Her forehead wrinkled and her eyes narrowed. Her water only twitched. She spent a long time on it. I worked on turning my candle on and off. I soon returned to my water, watching it swirl around. At last Aria managed to disturb her water further.

My head throbbed and I was ready to get out of the stuffy underground room. I wanted to see the light; there were no windows in the stone room. I wanted to breathe fresh air. The longer I stayed in that underground hideaway the more I was reminded of that filthy ship.

Another woman placed planted flowers in front of us. "Kill them," she said plainly. "Then bring them back." We looked at her stupidly. That would be bringing something dead back to life and I couldn't wrap my head around it. "You are in Lubelle's line, are you not? Then, do it!" Our helpers made us revive our plants, and then stir the air. They wanted us to levitate objects and more. When we were done for the day I felt so light headed I thought I was going to faint. We'd worked all day with no food or water or rest and still were barely able to do what they asked of us

"You did so well today. Tomorrow you'll do even better," Phyllis said as she saw us out the door. Even with her encouragements I felt pathetic. How could we ever defeat the powers of evil with these little magic tricks? How could we expect to develop our powers quick enough? As soon as I smelled food when we entered the inn all my worries washed away. I ate my beef quickly and hungrily and found myself dizzy with fatigue. Before I left for my room Barbara slipped me an envelope and due to the look she gave me I put it in my boot as to hide it from any untrustworthy eyes.

I sat on the bed and opened the unaddressed paper. There was a letter inside. I couldn't say that six words counted as a letter but it's all the same to me.

Same place. Same time. Come ready.

I fell back on my bed. How many more days of this training would I have to endure? How many *could* I endure? In a sense it was like the training many of the young men in Mar had to go through to become a soldier. The only difference was that all of our work was from our mind and I couldn't tell if that was better or worse.

Aria came in, "What did Barbara give you?" I lifted my hand and flailed the letter in the air. She laughed and snatched it. She wasn't laughing when she read it. She fell forward on to the bed. "They can't be serious," she mumbled miserably. I just groaned. "This sucks!" I had to laugh at her. Never had I heard her be so unladylike in my life.

I got up to lock the door and the window. Out in the gloomy street I could just see a lone walking figure. All I could see was his silhouette as he walked on. I could tell he was tall and lanky. Suddenly, he turned to my window. I couldn't see where he was looking but I felt that his eyes were on me. A shiver went down my spine like a cold knife barely sliding over the skin or like a drop of icy water on a steaming day. The hairs on the back of my neck stood alert. I made my fingers lock the window. Just when I was sure the figure would try to jump through my window from all the way down there and ring my neck he faded into nothingness. That's the first time I'd actually seen Samuel.

I closed the curtains and locked the door, "Aria, don't ever leave this room at night or leave anything unlocked." I remembered when Maria locked everything up for me that one night. When I looked to see if Aria was going to comment she was still lying on her stomach staring at me.

"You can feel it too can't you? Something's coming and I'm afraid it won't be good," I frowned.

"We're going to die." Her voice was haunted and accepting. "Both of us are. I can feel it." Her words made a petrifying image spring into my mind. I saw young beautiful Aria lying cold and still in a white laced coffin, her hands folded delicately across her chest. I lie next to her in a coffin of my own, just as silent. I forced back a shiver the gruesome picture caused.

"Aria, promise me you'll never say that again, promise! We are not going to die. Everything will be okay. We are the heroes and we can make it through this."

"Don't you remember that all of the heroes suffer greatly? I cannot promise anything to you, Reenie. It's easier not to hope, so when good does come it surpasses your expectations. It's easier to turn off all the lights so when a light does come on it is a relief. I do believe it is far easier than being disappointed."

"Aria . . . Promise me one thing? Please, promise me one simple thing," I begged her with my eyes. She didn't nod or make any sign of agreement. "Promise me that, even if we are destined to die, which we are not going to, you will not go out without a fight. Promise me that you will never give up." I wouldn't let Samuel win, not that easily. If he wanted our blood he was going to have to work for it.

She smiled a little and her eyes twinkled, "Now that, Renee, is a promise I can keep. I'll give him a run for his money." Her eyes filled with sadness again. "What do you think Mother and Father would say? Do you think that they'd be proud?"

"Well," I sat cross-legged beside her, "I think Father and Mother, both, would be proud. I think Mother would worry a great deal, especially knowing that there would be nothing she could do to stop us. I think Father wouldn't know what to do if he found out that his two little girls were witches, much less Mother being a witch. I believe he would try to stop us and I know he would fail. All the same he would be proud . . . I wish they were here, Aria. I've never wanted my mother so much."

"I've never wanted to sit in Father's lap so much before or lie in a safe bed," Aria went on with my complaining. "I just wish it didn't have to be so hard. I just wish it wasn't us."

I nodded in agreement, "Life sucks." We giggled at that and crawled into bed sleepily.

Pain Behind the Masks

Aria shook me awake the next morning, her face in a fright. "Reenie! Renee! Harro is at the door and he wants to see you. What do I do?" I jumped up and grabbed my hairbrush. "What do I do?!"

"I'm going to see what he wants. Wait for me downstairs with Barbara and Chene," I instructed. "If I'm not down in five minutes come and check on me." I opened the door calmly. Aria nodded politely and went to wait. "Harro, can I help you? It's barely morning?" I did not let him in.

"Yes, I'm sorry about that, but I wanted to apologize. I feel bad for the other night. I just have a heavy temper and whenever people speak of that stupid rumor, I tend to lose it. I never meant to hurt you," he took a long time to say nothing at all.

"I don't know if I can forgive you yet. And I'm not apologizing for striking you, if that's what you are waiting for." I tried to keep my voice level. I admit it was very hard between being angry, tired, and so scared I might've jumped from the window seal just to get away.

"No," he continued. "I would not have wanted you to. I was in the wrong and I very much deserved it and more."

"Is there anything else you would like to apologize for while you're here?" I asked snidely. He looked at me curiously and I took that as a no. Men, they can't remember a thing, can they? "I would think a gentleman would apologize for trying to seduce me when I was weak and defenseless. A gentleman would have apologized even when I wasn't weak and defenseless. To tell the truth I don't think a gentleman would have tried to seduce me at all. Yet, if my memory serves correctly, and it usually does, I had told you that you are not a gentleman. I've told you twice."

An emotion crossed his face that I could not identify quickly enough. If I had to guess, it was anger and hostility. "Yes, Renee, I am sorry for that too. However," he placed his hand under my chin, "you should be sorry. You are too beautiful for your own good. Your beauty makes my heart sorry that it cannot have yours. It makes my soul sorry that you do not want mine; and I am not sorry that you are so beautiful." He smiled at me. "Renee . . ."

"Thank you, Harro. I must be going now. Breakfast is waiting for me and chores for you." I walked by him and down to eat. It had taken a great amount of effort to keep from jerking away from him when he had touched me. His hand felt hot and charged with magic and the thoughts of what he could do that passed through my head were slimy and wretched. After knowing what he was I didn't think I could've held a conversation with him, but I did.

I *did* hold still when he touched me and I *did* walk away from him, all the while fearing that he would hurt me or kill me, or worse. I trotted down the stairs aware that my enemy was right behind me in the dark. I was taking a great risk, turning my back on him with no one around. I knew the only reason he did not cut me down where I stood was that Aria would know that he was the last to see me. He wouldn't be quick enough to stop her from accusing him and it would not take that much to convince the people that what she said was true. I counted my blessings when I got to the main room alive and unharmed.

Aria sat picking at a piece of sausage. She looked very worried, more so than the rest of the poor souls in the room. They looked tired and stressed. The loss of Luke touched even the coldest of hearts. Few laughed or smiled and the ones that managed to did so half-heartedly and gave up quickly. Deep purple bruises lay beneath their once bright eyes. Their minds were astray in deep thought and mourning over the young witch, one of the original lines of Tabitha Lenark.

I didn't know him well at all but by the looks of the heart broken people and their murmured words he was a great man. He had been kind and helpful, strong and hard working.

"He had a heart of gold."

"He was like a brother."

"He always helped out."

"He had so much life to live and so very much to offer. It was too soon."

"I only fear that his spirit will choose to stay among us. We already have two that should not be here. Another isn't going to help."

Luke was a genuine gentleman and a true man, or he had been. He was a prospering young boy, whose life was cut short by evil ones and by telling us the truth. Eating the food that Luke had always cooked in the kitchen must cause Aria more pain than I could ever know. She had been devastated by his loss. She tried not to show it so much but she didn't even have to say anything for me to know that his death cut her heart deep and left a wound that would never heal.

The food had lost its sweetness, void of the time and love Luke had cooked it with. The bacon under the egg eyes drooped and flopped about into a greasy frown. The eggs were lopsided and the yolk that oozed out was like yellow tears. They were tears of acid, burning holes in her heart and mind and her very soul. Aria had always liked certain men after a time or two of glancing at them, but Luke had been different. Form the moment she laid eyes on him she loved him. She felt whole and complete. A part of her had been filled that she didn't even know she had. Luke made her smile and laugh and act silly. She had blushed under his gaze and looked down shyly instead of batting her long lashes. Her light brown hair tossed with joy and her hazel eyes glimmered with gold. She had been happy and satisfied and completely content.

Now, in his absence, even though they only met for one night, she mourned for him more than the others ever could. The only one's pain she could not match was Luke's immediate family, and still she didn't fall too far. Her lips hung in a miserable frown. Her hair drooped and hung without attention. Her eyes were misty and the gold flecks in them appeared dull. Without him I feared she would never truly smile again, nor laugh or play. I dreaded the thought of those childish cheeks remaining pale forever. She might as well lie in a coffin. Her heart had died with young Luke and I don't think she even wanted it back if he did not come with it.

My heart broke for hers. Only someone who has a little sister could imagine the unbearable pain I went through when I saw my innocent Aria in such conditions. My heart was ripped into a thousand pieces as a heavy worded letter is torn to shreds by a teary-eyed maiden. I felt those slivers of myself freeze and die a little more.

I promised myself that if we made it through this battle I would take her somewhere bright. I would take her somewhere where the sun shined all day and the stars were bright. I would take her somewhere where flowers grew in snow and the rain smelled of their fragrance, where our weary bodies could rest in peace. Of course, we had to survive the havoc that lie ahead of us to reach that light. For now we were in a dark tunnel with no beginning and no end.

I sat by her, "Will you be okay?" I knew that she wasn't okay now but I hoped that she would be. She just nodded and nibbled on her breakfast meat. "Everything will turn out alright. It can't go on forever." She just sat there. I grabbed a fork and started eating too. I sighed and the air tasted of bitterness and sorrow. It was as if the world itself had stopped turning to mourn the loss of Luke. The earth itself cried out in pain and agony. The whole world cried. The plants in the windows that he had once watered drooped and curled in on itself as if to hold itself together. She sun seemed a bit duller now, its rays unable to warm our cold, broken hearts. The frilly clouds looked to be denser as if they were about to let their tears fall in honor of him. It was a traumatic day. The only one that did not look devastated was Harro.

Though he did not leap for joy or sing songs he did not mourn with the others. He may say that he did not know Luke well enough to mourn him, but I managed to. Aria certainly did. He may say that he wasn't social enough to comfort others. But Aria and I were strangers here and we had consoled them. The truth was that Harro didn't care that Luke had been cruelly murdered. He didn't care if any of us died. If I could guess, I would say that Harro and Samuel met Luke that night. Samuel had burnt his eyes. I was willing to bet that Luke had tried to use water against his foes but their fire had boiled it. A part of me knew Harro was the one who lit the steel bar with the fiery heat. I knew that he was the one who had mercilessly plunged it into Luke's chest. I knew he stood over Luke and listened to his screams, watching Luke die slowly.

I knew that Harro had watched Luke's soul leave his body and not even regret it.

Harro had no conscience, therefore he had no guilt. He had no sense of right or wrong other than that we were the enemy and his only ally was his dead father's spirit. Sadly that was all it took him to kill a young innocent fellow. He was nothing but a heartless bastard.

I put down my fork, having lost my appetite. "Aria, we have to go," I whispered.

She nodded her head, "We have to get out of here."

"No," I said wearily. "We have to go see Phyllis and the others."

"What? After everything, you're going to go through with this?"

"No, it's *because of everything* that I'm going through with this." I rubbed my head. "Luke can't have died in vain. You should know that. Plus, we can't leave Maria here to keep going on and on for another century. She deserves a rest." Aria started to interrupt me but I cut her off, "And the people, Aria. Just look at them. They are haunted by their past every day, especially when it catches up to the present. It needs to stop. It has to."

Aria just looked at me. "What did we do to deserve this?"

I couldn't answer her. I grabbed her hand and we walked out of the inn together.

"Hello," Phyllis greeted us half-heartedly. "We'll be working at Kari's today. Come along."

We walked over to old Kari's house, feeling as if we were on a wild goose chase for answers. "Ah, Renee. I'm so glad to see you again, dear," she greeted me. She led us past the front room and past the room where she told me that I would die soon. Beyond there was a house, plain and welcoming. She had cookies on the table and people roamed about. There weren't just elders this time. There were kids about my age all the way to people who looked like they were about to turn to dust.

"Renee, Aria, I'm so glad you came," Chene called to us. "I had to practically drag myself here but I suppose you two, and everyone else, did the same." We hugged and nodded. "Let me introduce you to some people." She walked into a group of young people, probably trying to help us make some friends. "This is Jacob, Brandon, Carry, Wanda, and Rick."

Jacob was a tall black man. His face was cleanly shaven and smiling brightly. He was strong under his plain white shirt and brown trousers. When we shook hands I noticed how firm and strong they were.

Brandon was a short boy with fluffy brown hair. He smiled very little and I recognized him as one of Luke's friends at the inn. His green eyes were still puffy from the news. Carry was a very short, young woman. She was blond with blue eyes and could make anyone laugh, even now, though I knew she must be tearing up inside.

Wanda turned out to be the woman with the cheating husband I had seen. Her black hair was short and straight. It framed her smiling face well but couldn't hide her stress.

Rick was very handsome though average. He was of average height with brown hair that went every which way. His eyes were the blue of the open ocean. His hands . . . were covered in bandages. I could only imagine how many fights he'd gotten into after hearing of Luke's death. I remembered seeing him with Luke as well as Brandon.

Everyone here tried to look happy, tried to look normal, but behind all of their hard efforts was a whole bunch of nothing. There was just a whole bunch of broken hearts in the room.

"I heard you just found out that you are witches," Jacob started to make small talk. "That must have been exciting."

I tried not to pinch my face in disgust, "No, not really."

Jacob just shrugged. "Sorry," Aria apologized for me. "It's just hard for us."

"Yes, I heard about your mother. I can only imagine what kind of burden this must be for you two. I just can't help but be happy that you chose this path, even though you are suppressing the feeling to scream and run the other way."

"No one lives forever." Aria's words brought the heavy reality of our lives crashing down on us once again. They all had the same knowing look on their faces. It was only then that I realized that Aria and I were not alone in facing the possibility of the ultimate end. We would not be the only ones to fight. We were not the only ones who might die. They chose, just as we did, to do the right thing. They willingly chose to stand behind us in our battle against evil. They chose their fate carefully and followed it. They would follow us. They were willing to die for us.

A new determination lit in me. I would not let these people down. I would not disappoint them. I felt angry for my self-pity and wallowing.

The room jumped and screamed. A glass of wine on Kari's table had exploded. The red liquid went everywhere along with the glass. Kari started cleaning up. "Renee, I'm afraid you are going to have to keep that temper of yours under control, not just hidden," she fussed at me.

"Excuse me?" I asked. "I wasn't even close to that glass. There's no way I could have hit it all the way from over here!"

"No, dear, you didn't hit the glass. I'm not that stupid. However, you still are to blame for shattering one of my better wine glasses." She threw away the glass slivers and wiped up the wine. "Surely, you know that your temper could cause things to happen. Just like when you splashed water everywhere right before Maria came to you. If I had to guess, there were other incidents as well."

She crooked a brow at me. "Can you think of none? Haven't you ever gotten mad at someone and they, so conveniently, slipped in a puddle of mud or tripped? Hadn't you been blamed for things that you couldn't have done because you were never in the room?" My wrinkled brow loosened in realization. "Ahh, that's what I thought. Now, get a grip on that temper young lady. It's time to begin training."

As we moved to her living room I thought others would frown at me and tell me that I wasn't worthy to be a witch. They only laughed and nodded. Rick winked at me and Carry smiled brightly. We all sat on Kari's couches or chairs that were centered around a table filled with dozens of lit candles. "Everyone needs to pick a candle," Kari instructed.

I want you all just to make it go out and come back on. Start now and do not stop until I tell you to do so.

I closed my eyes at the thought of more repetitiveness. Through my lids I saw many candles start to flicker off and on. They must belong to practiced witches. I took a deep breath and focused on my candle.

It was a pale blue with a white ribbon painted on it. As I saw it go out in my mind another light flickered off. I thought hard about it flickering on again. I imagined the wick exploding into flames. Nothing happened. I imagined someone lighting it again. Nothing happened. I sighed and just wished that it would light again. It did.

I opened my eyes to see it glowing. I closed my eyes, trying to think of how I did it. The more I forced the thought into life, the harder and more tiring it became. Instead I held the thought lightly in my head. My candle went off and on. It must be a state of just knowing what you want to do. You have to keep it simple. Magic couldn't be pressed.

I suppose it was like painting. The harder you tried the more of a mess you made. If you just held the picture in your head and let it flow gently from your mind to your hand and onto the canvas you could create a work of art. I continuously let my newly discovered magic flow from my head to my candle.

Eventually, my candle flickered on and off quickly. More and more did the same. After seeing Aria work her candle the day before, I could only imagine how she was doing now. Some were even shaping the flames.

"Stop," Kari told us. I opened my eyes as she got Jacob to carry in a large bowl of water. "Move the water, my children. Make it dip and rise every which way." She waited for us to do so. "Go on, go on! Close your eyes. We have no time to waste."

I closed my eyes again. Quickly I felt the water's power. It was cool and wet in a silky way. It was light and heavy, bright and dark. It was easier for me than with the fire. I opened my eyes, ready to test the water. Many others were making waves and dips. I stared at one particular spot and made the water tremble with the force of an unseen earthquake. It dipped to the bare bottom of the bowl then rose high above the rest. I formed a bubble under the water, making the liquid give room to the air. It rose to the surface with a small popping noise.

I concentrated completely on the water. I tuned out everyone's conversations. I tuned out all of the clattering, outside and within. The whole world disappeared and only the water and I remained. The water trembled and moved strangely. It moved away from the edges of the tin bowl. I wrinkled my brow. I caught Wanda's eye out of the corner of my own. She nodded her head, knowing what I was trying to do. She stared as I did, offering her help. I saw more and more do the same. This time the water easily rose from its bowl into the air to suspend over the table.

"Well done, my children. Many lessons have been learned quickly. Control the water. Levitate an item. Those are simple things to learn and to accept. Learning teamwork takes time. The power of those around you can aid your cause. Focusing on one thing together makes things much easier. Many can move a mountain, while only one can move a grain of sand." Together we lowered the clear water back to its holder and kept on individually.

"You learn quickly, young ones. You must continue to do so." She brought in plants. She brought in everything from weeds to daisies, carnations to roses, and set them throughout the room. "You know what to do."

I focused on a small pink carnations Kari helped the others. I tried to hold the thought of it wilting lightly in my mind, but I couldn't do it. The thought of killing something so beautiful was disgusting to me. Then I remembered how beautiful I had thought Harro to be. I once thought him to be an angel but he was only a demon. I knew I would have to kill that beautiful man . . . so I killed those gorgeous carnations.

Their beautiful, sunset pink crinkled and turned a ghastly brown. Its green leaves dried and rolled in on themselves. I felt Kari's hand on my shoulder and her lips at my ear. "Compassion is neither fault nor weakness. It is a virtue that can only make you stronger." She patted my back and walked away.

I smiled, happy to know that my love for the flowers was not a bad thing. I remembered how they had been before and the flowers breathed in life once again. Their leaves were brighter than ever and their petals a richer pink. Death can only take so much from one. No matter what happened its beauty would live on. I could only hope that if I died my legacy would live on as well. I practiced over and over again, each time the hurt of killing the flower was as strong as the last, but I knew that killing another human being would be much harder, so I kept on.

A HAPPY MOMENT

Kari had us repeat all three lessons over and over. For hours we carried on. My head hurt so much that I had to wipe away tears but I kept trying. At times I thought my head would explode. At times I wished it would, just to relieve some pressure, just to make it stop for a while. I pushed myself as far as the others until Kari asked us to stop. Silently she took away the water. She put her plants back in place. She spread her candles out again. While we waited for her some of us chatted. Some of us rested our eyes. I rubbed my head.

Rick came and sat by me, "It will get easier. I remember when I couldn't get a candle to light without spraying everyone with hot wax. Now, it is a piece of cake. I promise, it won't always be this hard."

"Somehow I can't believe that," pressed my temples. It didn't help very much. Actually, it didn't help at all.

"Let me see," Rick took my hand. He turned it palm up and rubbed. As he did he spoke peacefully, "When I was a boy I always got terrible migraines. They would get so bad that I could only stay in bed for days until Mother convinced Kari to come and help me. One day Kari showed

Mother how to cure my headaches. She told my mother to rub my palm and have nothing in mind but good thoughts. After a while I stopped having headaches of that kind. I haven't had one since."

I closed my eyes and listened to his voice and the throbbing in my head faded away. "Of course," he chuckled and set down my palm, "Kari can always *cause* a headache." We laughed. "Thank you."

"What are you thanking me for? I should be the one thanking you," I said. "Thank you."

He smiled, "Your welcome." His smile stayed in place but his eyes grew sad, "Thank you for coming. You have no idea what that means to me and everyone else. It gives us a little hope to hold on to."

"What else could I have done? Leaving behind all this mayhem when we're supposed to be fixing it is not an option."

"You'd be surprised at how many hopeful heroes have fled this town." He looked at me, "Then again, I guess that's what makes hero. You didn't run." I smiled back at him not saying how much I had wanted to and still wanted to.

"Congratulations, apprentices," Kari's old voice boomed to us. "You've worked hard and deserve a rest. Go home to your houses. Eat. Sleep. Tomorrow the true test begins. Will you be strong enough to return? I do hope so," she bowed her head in her dramatic scene. "Farewell." She left us to show ourselves out. We poured out little by little, trying to avoid making a scene on the streets.

Aria and I walked sluggishly back to our new home, that wretched old inn. People grinned at us openly now instead of glancing at us accusingly. I didn't even bother to look twice. As soon as we walked through the door Barbara was setting food out for us. I didn't know what it was and, frankly, I couldn't have cared even if I had wanted to. I just knew it was warm food that could fill my belly. Barbara asked us no questions, though I was sure she knew where we had been. I suspected she would know everything as soon as she had a private moment to talk to her mother, Chene.

I ate quickly, not caring if I seemed savage. All I knew was that I had worked hard, harder than men at work had, and I deserved a meal. I nodded thanks to our dear Barbara and made my way up to the room. I felt light headed and heavy in the middle. I was fat and happy and ready for a fit sleep, no matter it was only in the mid afternoon. I closed the door behind me. I checked that the window was locked and no one was lurking in our quarters. With my lids already half closed I removed my boots. I didn't even remember crawling under the covers and resting my head on my pillows as I surrendered to sleep immediately.

In my dreams I dreamt of when Father died and Mother was taken. Everything was so vivid. It was exactly what I had hoped to avoid. But I was numb to all the emotions I had suffered through. My slumber was too deep to feel anything.

HIDE AND SEEK

Morning came slowly, and that was good—very good, indeed. I woke drowsily, hardly noticing that Aria was gone from bed. I barely cared that she was gone from the room. I brushed my hair slowly and smoothly, still in a daydream haze. I changed to a day dress and walked to my bathroom. I splashed cold water on my face and finally managed to become fully aware. Maria was there in my mirror, but she didn't frighten me. She just waved and smiled and vanished like before. She must be checking in on me.

The dead, dark-haired woman had quickly become a friend. She helped and guided me just as one would. At some point she had seemed like an older sister, making sure I was safe all the time. Now she started to feel like a mother. Her eyes had that look in them that just made you think "Mama". She checked in on me as my mother used to when I was a young child. It wasn't always from fear that you would be taken, that you would run away, that you would need her; it was just that motherly instinct.

Of course, Maria had been a mother. She had born and raised four beautiful, powerful children. Though one turned out to be a rotten egg and she would never get the chance to see her three daughters achieve the best in life, she was a mother and always would be.

Surprisingly, I wasn't offended by her intrusion in that part of my life. Knowing she was there was quite comforting.

But where was Aria? Her boots were gone and her nightdress was folded neatly on our wardrobe. I couldn't recall feeling her rise from the bed or hear her change and leave. I was too far lost in one of the best sleeps of my life, despite reliving the worst night of my life, to notice anything. The world could have ended in my slumber and I would never have known.

I trotted down the steps to see if Aria was there. I spotted Chene cleaning a table and went up to her. "Chene, you wouldn't have possibly seen Aria this morning, would you?"

"Actually, I did. She rose early and ate. Last time she spoke to me she said she was going to get some fresh air. I haven't seen her since and that must have been at least a half hour ago," she told me. "I'm sure she couldn't have gone far, dear."

"Thank you," I smiled and stepped outside. It still amazed me at how quaint this little town was. In Mar we'd all had our own homes; they weren't piled on top of one another, except for the inns, of course. The streets had been wide for the bulky vehicles to pass by. The sidewalks were always packed with thick foot-traffic. Sometimes it was so thick it spilled into the road and caused mayhem for those in their automobiles.

Here it was still fairly thick, but not nearly as troublesome, mainly in part of the courtesy and respect these people had towards one another. And in Mar I had never looked to the sky except to point out what shapes the clouds had chosen to take that day. Here, in little, old Roe, I could look up and breathe deeply.

The skies were blue and open with great, white, puffy clouds lacing through it. The sun was bright and warm on my face. The smell of fresh fields drifted to my nose. I felt whole and open here, where the sky seemed to open your heart with its miraculous beauty.

I looked up and down the street, not knowing which way Aria would have taken. I went right, to the market. I did not see her in the crowd of hungry people. She wasn't studying the strange fruit or testing their delicious pies. I moved on to the bookshop. Phyllis was there, "Good morning, Renee. Our meeting isn't until later."

"Good morning, Phyllis. I know. I was just looking for Aria. She rose before I did and didn't bother to leave a note."

"I haven't seen her this way, but you might try at Kari's. I think Aria likes her very much."

"Thank you," I nodded and left with the little doorbell tinkling a good bye to me. I searched the streets as I strode to Kari's house. I liked Kari too and wouldn't doubt to find her there. As our tutor, Kari had a strong hold on us already. If I could, I would just stop by and talk to her at times. It would be nice just to chat and nothing more. However, the location of my little sister was still an unknown thing.

Kari opened her door before I could even raise my fist to knock, "I'm sorry, dear, I haven't seen her this morning."

"Oh, uhm," I didn't know what to say. "Do you know where she might be?"

"Well, I thought it would be obvious. You've scavenged this side of town and she's nowhere to found. Logically, you will find her on the other side."

I laughed at her use of common sense and sarcasm, "Thank you, Kari. I'll see you later." I waved to her and retraced my steps. I passed the library and the market and finally the inn. I was hoping for Kari to give me more specifics on Aria's whereabouts. The only place that I knew of over here was Maria Lenark's abandoned home and I knew Aria would not dare tread on that ground. I was left to walk slowly down the street and ask a person once in a while if they had seen my sister. Most of them had not, but they tried to soothe me.

"No, Miss, I haven't seen her. Then again I haven't been looking for her. All these girls start to look the same when you pass them on the street. She can't have wondered too far." I also passed the red-headed man in his big coat but was too intimidated to speak to him as he strode by in his big boots.

The few people that had seen her kept me walking further on. I didn't think I would ever find her and thoughts of returning to the inn to let her find me started to become a serious option. Then, I heard her laugh. I looked across the street that was now empty because we were on the very outskirts of town. She was there with two other girls.

They both had glossy auburn hair that was cropped just above their shoulders. They only looked to be a few inches differing in height.

They were twins.

Aria caught sight of me and waved me over, "Renee, this is Meagan and Drew. Girls, this is my sister, Renee." The one she pointed out as Meagan was about three inches shorter than her twin was, she had fewer freckles and her eyes were a brighter green. She looked to be strong and powerful, but what would I know about that?

The other sister, Drew, was tall. She had many light freckles littering her face and her green eyes almost seemed grey. She looked frail, but a part of me knew that she was very practiced in her magic. I knew she was a fighter.

They both smiled at me, "It's nice to meet you." They giggled at chiming the words at the same time.

"It's nice to meet you, too," I grinned. I turned to Aria and spoke lightly, "I've been looking for you everywhere. You didn't even let Chene know where you would be so she could let me know."

She just shrugged. "I didn't know where I would be or how long I'd be gone. I started wondering around and I met Meagan and Drew. We've just been talking for a while and they've been showing me some of the things they've learned to do."

Meagan nodded. "Would you like us to show you a few things?" She sounded awkward talking to me. I guessed that she did not wish to seem rude. She didn't want to act like a know-it-all and be overpowering when she must have been at least two years younger than I was, maybe three. I smiled and nodded.

She bit her lip and looked around. She stared at the leaves in the street that swirled and danced slowly to the songs of the light wind of which we could never hear. They floated up into a ball that hovered three feet from the ground. I watched as they bobbed there quietly as a lightning bug will at night. They started spinning rapidly and a sudden outburst of wind distorted them. They floated back to the street and continued to prance along.

I was about to compliment Meagan on her exquisite display but she cried out first. "What was that for?" I thought she was talking to me but I turned back to her to see her sharp face glaring at her sister's. "You always do that, you little pest!"

"Well, you're always such a show off!" Drew struck back.

"At least I don't ruin your shows!"

"That's because you're older and think it matters," Drew said simply. "If I were older I'd do the same thing. Now you blame it on my peskiness and jealousy. If I were older you'd think I was overpowering and rude."

"It's not a matter of me be older or younger than you, it is a matter of courtesy and respect. You can be so foolish," Meagan scowled upwards to her younger twin sister's face. "Never mind that now, we're being rude and shameful in front of our new friends. Forgive us."

Aria laughed, "That's quite all right. We know all about sisterly squabbles. Though I can't say we've ever had quarrels over magic before. It's mainly been over whose turn it is to do the dishes and who left the gate on the hen house unlatched."

We all laughed.

"Drew, Meagan, do you think you two will be joining us?" I asked and they didn't seem to understand. "*You know* . . . ?"

"Oh, that!" Meagan whispered.

"Actually, yes. Word had just reached us late yesterday afternoon. We plan to go today." Drew spoke proudly, a true witch.

"Good, I think you two would do better than excellent." I smiled.

"Speaking of which," Aria looked to the sky to gauge what time it was, "we'd better be off to get ready. We'll see you there." We all waved good-bye and departed. As Aria and I walked back to the inn for lunch I tried to concentrate on the leaves in the street. I wanted to levitate a whole bunch of them as Meagan had, but they only puffed and heaved. I could tell that the next days at Kari's house would be tiresome and hard worked.

Chene smiled to us secretively as we ate her fried chicken with white gravy and green beans. The taste of their food always coated my tongue in their brilliant flavors. I couldn't help but eat every morsel on my plate.

When Harro entered the room from the back I acted as if I had not seen him. He approached us at the bar, but before he reached us I swallowed the last bit of my meal, grabbed Aria's hand and fled out the door. I was careful not to look fearful of him. I just tilted my head to the sky and hoped that it gave him the impression that I would not talk to him after everything he had done. I still could barely believe that he was Samuel's immortal son.

Reality crashed in on me again as I remembered that he'd been so awful and rude: he'd hurt my arm, and tried to seduce me twice—three times, if you counted the time he'd bought me a rugan cake, kissed my hand, and had that terrible, hungry look in his eye.

There was no doubt he was Samuel's son.

He tried to win me over in the simplest way and had pushed me away in those same ways. He reeked of a dark loathsome energy. The vibes that were produced from somewhere inside his chiseled body was like a flashing sign that read: *Beware. Caution. RUN.* It was him all right, and I could not deny that.

LESSONS AND
OBSERVATIONS

I kept shooting glances over my shoulder to make sure he wasn't following us. I didn't see him so we kept on to the short journey to Kari's home, where dozens of people would be waiting for us. I hoped to see Meagan and Drew and all the friends I had met yesterday. I knew I would not see Chene. It would be too hard for her to leave her work every afternoon, not to mention that Harro would notice quickly. Again, the door was opened before we ever knocked and we stepped through the doorway swiftly. We went and sat with the other people.

Rick and Jacob waved from across the room and yelled a hello. It was okay that no one approached me; I was too nervous to make small talk and much too distracted. Thankfully, Kari soon started the session.

She raised her hands, "Silence, my children. Peace and hear me." Her voice was strong and echoed through her house. "The elements must be tamed but we must move on from them. Practice at your own leisure while we move along to harder tasks here. Telekinesis, moving objects with your mind, is one of the best ways to defend yourselves and to be offensive. Why is that?" she asked the crowd.

Wanda was the one to speak up. "If someone is sending a spell at you, or another object, you can block it with an object of your own. You could also move objects toward your enemy. You could throw rocks at them or branches and such. If you are strong enough you can even move your enemy."

"Good, good. Take an object and place it in front of you. Preferably something that's not breakable!" she shouted. I set my emptied cup on the floor in front of me.

"Concentrate. Silence the world around you and move your item. Do not become frustrated too quickly; it will all come in time."

Before I could even concentrate on my glass Meagan had moved the hands on one of Kari's many noisy clocks. I shook my head, reminding myself that I had only just begun when Meagan had probably been doing this for years.

I focused on my cup and blocked everything out. That part was easy. After watching and seeing so much death and hearing so many things that you wished you had never heard, as I had, you learned to tune things out quickly. I knew that the others were still around me but they faded in to the background while my cup became the main objective in my vision. The hard part was actually forcing action onto my drinking glass.

I tried yesterday's method of holding the thought lightly in my mind and merely seeing it happen. The cup remained still and silent. I tried over and over again thinking I had maybe somehow lost my connection. But nothing happened. I tried to force the thought, I pushed it until I thought it would burst, but nothing happened. I sighed, confused, but not yet losing my patience. I thought to myself as I kept my eyes on the goblet, *What am I doing wrong? The magic was fairly easy yesterday and the day before. I could catch on then. What's wrong with me? Is something wrong with the glass? I wish you would just move!*

I startled. Did my cup just move? It couldn't have, but I was sure that it was a hair to the left. I grabbed my cup and lined it up with two lines in the rug; a red line on the right and a black line underneath. That way if it moved again I would know for sure. But what had I done to make it move? Had it really even budged at all? Yes, it had. What had I thought to the cup?

I tried getting mad at the immobile cup—I had been very annoyed with it. It did not budge an inch. I sighed and thought, *Move, please, move.* And it did! It moved a whole two carpet lines to the left. *Move.* It fell over. I didn't want it to fall over. I had wanted it to keep moving to the left . . . *Move left.* It rolled on its side to the left.

This was going to be tiring; I was going to have to tell it every move I wanted it to make. *Stand up. Move left. Bump in to Aria.* Aria looked up and narrowed her eyes at me. Then she saw the cup. *Move right. Come back to me.* Aria scowled at me and became transfixed on her coin again. I looked up to see Kari smiling approvingly at me. I smiled back and returned to my glass. *Roll to Jacob's foot, but stop before you hit him.* It did not move.

What had I done wrong this time? Perhaps my instructions did not seem clear enough. *Roll right before Jacob's foot. Do not bump into it.* I watched it roll and wiggle roughly across the carpet and stop an inch before hit Jacob's foot.

I looked at Jacob. He was as fine and handsome as he had been the day before. Except, he now had a look in his eye. He was completely focused on the marble that floated in the air before him. His eyes seemed a little glassy but they were strangely clear, like a sinner seeing God for the first time.

He smiled a little mischievously and made his orange marble bump into Brandon's green one. Brandon scolded Jacob when his green marble fell to the ground with a thud. He slowly raised it to eye level again when Jacob's orange marble started to move towards it again. Brandon tried to move his out of the way but, still, it fell. He looked to be growing impatient.

His marble rose another time, his jaw locked in concentration. As his friendly opponent's marble moved closer I thought, *Levitate. Capture the orange marble. Don't touch the green marble.* I shook with silent laughter at the look on Jacob's face. My cup had turned upside down and landed over his marble. I could hear the stone marble clank against the smooth wood of my cup, now unable to move in its little prison.

Though he was older than I was, Jacob childishly stuck his tongue out at me while Brandon smiled and snickered. I smiled triumphantly but released the orange marble and let my cup fall. Now that I listened the room was filled with a symphony of thuds and clanks.

I had a joyous time, moving my cup about. Aria got her coin into the air, but sometimes she would lose the connection and I would catch it in my glass. This dearly annoyed Aria to her wits end. She finally threw the little silver coin at me. Right before it hit my nose it stopped. I gasped when I realized I had made it stop. I was amazed at how it floated before me and my cup still hovered by my knee. I hadn't thought loudly for it to halt. It had been more of a silent command, but the coin still took heed. It was like when you simply moved your arm. You don't have to think *stretch* to your arm; it just happens because your brain wants it to. A smile crept across my face as I returned the coin to Aria and set the cup on the ground.

Few noticed my new discovery, but those who did kept an eye on me during my experiments. Down the hall I could see Kari's personal water pump, from where I sat. My cup floated down the hall to it and as soon as it knew what I wanted I held the cup under its faucet. Slowly, the pump started to do its job. Cool, fresh water was pumped into my cup. I made the rusty pumping stop as my cup obeyed my thoughts and commands and came back to me.

I caught it in my hand and took a sip, as if to make sure it was really there. Some smiled at me and returned to their work. Most of the witches in the roomed looked down right bored. No doubt they'd already mastered this trick and were merely amusing themselves by rotating their objects or casting them across the room. I was fascinated.

Telekinesis came easy to me, just like the element of water had. I gave Aria a sideward glance; she had gotten the hang of it now and the coin was whirring so fast in the air that it made a whooshing sound with a high pitch behind it. Kari watched each person, giving them a quick over look, but she had watched me closely during my discovery. All the while my cup had drifted down her hall, filled, and drifted back her eyes were on me. Her gaze did not follow my steady glass nor did it transfer to anyone else during that time. I knew she was examining me.

She was watching for my reaction, my control, and so on. She didn't seem displeased; she simply wore her unreadable mask. Now that I was through, her eyes scanned over the others again as if nothing had happened.

As I finished my water then rolled my cup around (with my mind now, of course) I examined the others in the room.

Jacob was lounging in his claimed cushioned chair. His marble wrote strange symbols in the air and did figure eights. I envied him. Even as his eyes drooped lower and then back up, but always down again, he had complete control. He even dodged Brandon's marble as it tried to knock his off course. Even as he dozed in and out of consciousness and a little dribble of drool hung on his lip, I envied him.

He looked a mess, no doubt working a night job. He looked ruffled and was unshaven. Big, dark bags were starting to form under his eyes. Those dark, full brown eyes. His hands were scratched from work, but still I envied him. Yes, he looked absolutely horrid, but he was also still a beautiful sight to behold. His body was long and strong, covering over six feet of height and plenty wide enough. If I were to put my hand up to his it would be like putting an infant's hand up to mine.

His unshaven jaw was hard and square. His teeth were white and fairly straight. He was like a great lion; wild and untamed. He was strong and could act quickly despite his façade of relaxation and drowsiness. He was beautiful. You just couldn't deny that.

Carry stood in a corner, making a flower sway from side to side in a slow dance. Her blonde hair glowed gold and her blue eyes looked icy. Though she was young, she was tall. Maybe she only seemed to be tall. Even in the depths of fatigue she put her shoulders back and her chin up. She held her back straight as if an iron rod was supporting her.

She reminded me of the dancers in Mar that would scurry all over the theater stage. They would prance and skip in their brightly painted dresses. Yet inside I knew she

120

still wasn't over the loss of Luke, no one was and probably never would be. Nonetheless, she was here and she was trying and for that I saluted her.

Dear, short Wanda played mentally with the frills of one of Kari's throw pillows. Though no windows were let open and there was no draft it appeared to be that there was a phantom wind blowing about the frills. Her short, black hair was strangely still as if she had weights on the end of it. Now that I looked more closely, she did! Here and there were little metallic beads keeping her hair straight. In the candle light her eyes looked to be golden yellow framed by thick lashes. I couldn't see behind the mask she kept about her face so I assumed she was dealing well with her unfaithful husband and backstabbing sister.

Rick moved a chain on the table and fiddled with a bit of leather around his neck. The chain he moved was a gold necklace, plain and simple with a locket attached. He kept opening it and closing it, as if hoping that whatever was there would be different.

Like Jacob he was handsome, but in a different way. Jacob had a draw about him. Rick was simple and kind and set off good vibes. People appeared to feel safe around him. Yes, he was average. Yes, he was quiet. Yes, he did not stand out in a crowd, but he was handsome. His brown hair just barely drooped into his eyes—those eyes! Like Jacob's they were enticing, but Jacob's had been nearly black. Rick's eyes were a clear, clear blue. There were no flecks in them at all. It was just a solid pale blue.

I had to watch him in my peripheral vision to observe him. His eyes kept scanning the room; he acted like someone kept whispering his name.

Poor, Brandon. Yesterday I hadn't bothered to look at him really. His hair was short and a fluffy light brown that he wore as if he had just woken up. His aura was like that too. He was the laid back, funny guy. He was the one that you always expected trouble from, like Lance Banks, our class clown in Mar.

However, I noted that his looks were quick and sharp. Inside, he stood on edge, always waiting for something to come up. He kept trying to get his marble to hit Jacob's but they never connected or collided with each other. His eyes kept wandering to the same corner so, I followed his gaze to see what he thought was so interesting. I almost laughed. He was staring at the twins: Meagan and Drew.

Drew was very powerful. I noticed that she was moving many things at once: a clock, a stray ribbon, and a candle. As I had expected earlier, she was not frail. She only appeared to be, with her charm and slender fingers. She stood tall and proud without seeming to try or even notice.

I wished to be her. She was beautiful with her short, glossy, auburn hair. It was like the embers of a fire. A thought popped into my head. Drew was a tiger. She was beautiful and at times could look small and frail when she was laid back in the shade. At the same time she was fast and powerful and cunning. I'm sure she had claws and that she would use at a moment's notice. Her smoky grey eyes held all this truth.

Her sister Meagan was just as beautiful. Her hair was the same but looked a bit softer. Her green eyes wandered about the room, all the while still moving objects. But she was not I tiger. The feeling I got from her was that from a sly house cat. Those green eyes watched everything as if it were prey that she would eventually kill. For now she was only observing their game, studying and watching. All the same she was as powerful as her younger sister was and could be just as dangerous.

I think Kari sensed it, too. I don't know how I knew. Maybe it was that Kari's eyes kept slipping back to young Meagan. Maybe it was that Kari avoided Meagan and doted on Drew when we conversed. Perhaps it was the look in Kari's eyes when she looked at Meagan: wariness and suspicion.

It was the look you gave a snake that lay curled up and unmoving on the side of the road. Maybe it was just instinct, but somehow I knew that old Kari did not completely trust Meagan as she did Drew and Jacob and Rick and the others. I would trust Kari's instincts even if I didn't know why. Though she was old and wrinkled, and I was sure she was frailer than she acted to be, I would trust her.

My eyes returned to my cup that was spinning 'round and 'round on the carpeted floor. I enjoyed observing my peers. It was good to collect information about those around me. Knowledge is power. I would collect all the knowledge I could. I would watch more and listen harder. Mother had always taught me that eavesdropping was wrong but I would do that too if it meant that I could find out more.

Knowledge was the most powerful thing right now, even more so than abilities to control magic. I would watch my companions, townspeople, and even my sister.

Most of all I knew I had to keep an eye and an ear for Harro. The more we knew about him and any plans he might have the better a chance we would have of fighting him.

My eyes drifted to Aria, sweet Aria with her light brown hair and hazel eyes. I would have to watch her, too. I would have to keep an eye on her and watch who she was talking to and being with. I would have to become Mother, watching her every move, not to be mean or intrusive, but to protect her. I had to protect her from others . . . and from herself, her ever curious self.

VISIONS AND SORROWS

I heard a thud and jumped. Jacob had finally fallen asleep and his orange marble now dropped to the floor, causing the ominous sounding thud. He didn't move at the sound. His head rested on his fist and his jaw hung loosely. Every muscle in his body was lax. I was almost afraid his long body would slide out of his chair. His chest rose and fell with his deep, steady breathing. Not a single sign of awareness flitted behind his closed lids.

I smiled at his resting body. Mentally, I lifted his marble and set it on the table quietly, so as he could find it. The rest of us in the room returned to our lesson, some of them were now whispering back and forth to each other and keeping their objects moving too.

I just watched Jacob's peaceful body become heavier and heavier. Though he was older than I was, he was childish and innocent in his rest. All of his worry and stress fell away leaving only a tired man. Then, he twitched. It was nothing more than that and I had seen Aria do in her dreams before. He twitched again. Then, again but more violently. His muscles clenched as if he was having a bad dream. His breathing grew rough and his face squinted.

I got up, leaving my cup still, and went to him. "Jacob?" I said, not daring to touch him. When Mother woke Father from dreams like this he woke up swinging. He would apologize until the end of the world and she would say that it wasn't his fault, but she still got hit. I could only imagine being hit by Jacob's big hands with the power of his huge body behind them. I shook my head, "Jacob, wake up!" He kept on with his nightmare . . . and it got worse. His nostrils flared and he pushed back into his seat. Now there were more people telling him to wake up and so on. "Jacob," I said again.

Meagan rolled her eyes at me. "Jacob," she grabbed the arm that was still holding his head up. Before she could say any more his hand closed around her wrist and his eyes popped wide open. Those eyes were huge and the whites were bloodshot. He didn't act as if he saw her, or anyone else. He stared on at something we could not see.

He jumped and jolted in fear or pain. I could tell that his grip on Meagan's wrist kept getting tighter and now she yelled out in pain, "Ow! Jacob, let me go! You're hurting me!" She went down to her knees.

"Out of my way!" I heard Kari fussing her way through the crowd. "MOVE! Jacob?" she looked into his unseeing eyes. She put her hands on the one that was gripping Meagan. "It is okay, Jacob," she spoke clearly. "Release her. It is okay. Release Meagan." Slowly, ever so slowly, Jacob loosened his grasp and finally let go to grip the arm of his chair until I heard the creak of wood beneath the cushions.

Kari put her hands on Jacob's shivering, sweating face. "Jacob, come back to us. Come back to me. Turn away from what you see, child. Close your eyes against the evil you see." Kari never blinked as she spoke. "It is okay, young

Jacob. Come home to us. Walk away from what you see, but remember the warning. Bring us back a message."

Jacob stopped moving all at once. His deep, brown eyes closed and his sweat stopped pouring. He became completely still and I thought he might've been dead, except that he was still breathing. "Jacob?" Kari whispered. The man's eyes opened slowly and tiredly. "What did you see?"

"Oh, Kari," he whispered back. I had a feeling that he could not have managed more than that slight whisper of breath.

"What, Jacob? What did you see?" Kari was patient and clear.

"It was everywhere. It was in the streets and on the houses and in front of our doorsteps. It was awful. Oh, Kari, who could have done such a thing?"

"Who could have done what? Jacob I need you to tell me. What was everywhere?"

"Red, Kari. Red rose petals." The entire room gasped at his words.

Kari's face was grave and worried. She left the room and came back. "Drink this, it will help." She handed Jacob a thick brew and he drank. His eyes started to droop again and soon he was back in a dreamless slumber.

"That's right my child, rest your soul and your eyes." She took the cup from his hand and set it on the table. She took the time to look every one of us in the eye. When she met me her eyes were solemn and full of shadows, and that look sent a shiver of ice down my spine and froze my heart in mid-beat.

She finally spoke, weary and regretful, "Now, you know. Now, you know what you are up against. This is not a child's game of tag or hide-and-seek. This is real. And yes it is scary. The fear of what is to come shakes my soul . . .

and I see that it does yours as well. Whoever plans to do this will take no mercy with us.

"Now you know." Her voice started to grow louder and somewhat exasperated with this whole situation. "Now you know why I push you so hard. You need to be pushed. Time is not on our side. Time is unknown to us. We cannot control it. So we must make the most of it. We cannot let Samuel win. If we do I fear that this world of ours will end. Roe will be no more."

She turned to me, "Every time I try to look down the possible future path where Samuel wins this war I see only black nothingness. I take that as the end of me or the end of all of us. The future is dark, my dears. Hold your light high and proud and return tomorrow to continue to let it to shine." She bowed her head and walked into the back of her house to pace.

The room was tense and silent after she left. None of us moved or whispered a word for a long while. We all stood in silence with our heads bowed, as if in prayer. And I knew some of us were. If what Jacob saw came true . . . I don't know what would happen. I had only been here a little while but I still understood what a red rose meant. Knowing that and imagining their petals all over the city was horrible.

Drew was the one to speak through a thick voice, "When we leave we must do so as every other day. We must leave little by little." Everyone nodded in agreement and I noticed Meagan rubbing her arm where there would be a bruise.

"We can't let anyone know what happened here," Rick managed to say. "Act normal and say nothing." We nodded again and people started to leave a few at a time.

I went over to Rick who sat on the floor by Jacob. "Will he be okay?"

Rick looked up with his blue eyes. "I wouldn't know, but I hope that he will be."

I sat down in front of him while those blue eyes followed me. "I'm sorry," I apologized.

"What are you apologizing for?" he tilted his head up to look at his dreaming friend. "That wasn't your fault. It just happened. He's done that a few times before. Not that bad, but still . . . it wasn't your fault."

"I know," I looked down. "I'm still sorry about Jacob. You two must be great friends."

He smiled a little. "We've been friends since grade school. I can't remember how we met but I can remember that we did everything together. We've learned together, fought together, and played together. He's a loyal friend." I nodded. He looked across the room to the door and I was afraid that he was waiting for me to go. "Your sister just left."

"She needs some time alone," I said. My sister and I were very alike in this measure. When we were upset we didn't like to be pushed and crowded and cuddled. Sometimes we just needed to be alone.

He nodded, "I know how that can be."

"Would you like me to leave?" I asked, amazed that I kept the sorrow out of my voice.

"No, no," he said. We were quiet for a while, neither of us knowing what to say. "You must be scared out of your wits."

"Aren't you?" I raised my brows

"I hate to admit it but I am. I'm scared for myself and my friends and my family." He played with his necklace. He fidgeted with it, lacing it through his fingers.

"What is that?" He gave me a curios look. I asked more clearly, "Is that a locket of some sort?"

129

He looked down, "Ah yes . . ."

"I'm sorry, I didn't mean to intrude. It just seems to make you sad."

"That's okay," he shook his head. He opened the small locket and handed it to me. "That's my sister, May."

"She's very beautiful," I said, and she was. The young girl in the picture was slight and blonde. Her yellow-green eyes were held high on distinct dimples. She looked so bright and happy. "I don't think I've seen her." I passed his necklace back to him.

He stared at May's picture as he spoke to me. "You wouldn't have. She died two years ago. That's when Harro first arrived here. She hadn't been ill or troubled." He sighed deeply, "We found her near Maria's house. She had been poisoned . . . she had only been eighteen."

I could feel his sorrow. It was so strong I could hardly breathe. "I'm so sorry." He closed his locket and looked up to me. "I kind of know how it feels. I'm supposed to have another sister and a brother. Lilly and Michael died in birth. The loss is great; greater even for you since you knew your sister. I'm—"

"Please don't," he took my hand. "It was long ago. I know I'll never get over it but I've moved on." He looked down at my small hand in his large one and hurriedly released it.

"How have you been holding up?" he changed the subject.

"Fairly well, I suppose. As best as I could expect myself to hold up. I just hope everything turns out okay." I didn't reveal to him the feeling I had that told me it might not.

"So do I. There are many things I still want to do," he looked into the distance. He shook his head, "I think you'd better find your sister. Brandon and I are going to wait here until Jacob wakes up."

I stood up and wiped off my dress, "Good-bye, Rick."

"I'll see you tomorrow, Renee," he called as I slipped out the door. He was very kind and a good friend. I hoped I would see him tomorrow. I hoped I'd get to see him the day after that and then after that. I hoped I'd get to continue to get to see all of my new friends in Roe. But if Jacob's vision came true I may not get to keep them.

FINDING AND FACING

I shook my head to clear my thoughts and put on a normal face; I had a feeling that I'd been brooding. I made my face was light and innocent, though it was hard to keep that way. I was about to pass the inn when Chene ran out to me.

"Renee, I don't know where Aria is," she grabbed my elbow and whispered. "I saw her pass the inn and when I stepped out and called for her she just kept walking! What's happened?"

I looked around then whispered back, "Jacob had a vision. It was bad, Chene, very bad. There were red rose petals all over the town." Chene gasped and I nodded. "You said she passed the inn?"

"Yes, she just kept on walking."

"I'm going to go find her. If she comes back, keep her here." I took off to the end of town knowing Chene would do as I asked.

What was Aria thinking? Was she insane? After everything with Jacob this afternoon I thought she would have been smarter than to wonder off. I guess not. As I walked through the town I watched for her and asked if anyone had seen her. The few people that had seen her pointed me further and further on to Maria Lenark's house like earlier.

What if she had gone into the house? Samuel would be there for sure and probably Harro if he was able to get away from town. She wouldn't survive if she made it in. Come to think of it she would die right there in Maria's garden. The evil flowers would become creatures. I could see it in my mind. They would creep towards her and bind her with their thorny stems that were so like barbwire. She would feed them her own unwilling blood. I shivered and kept walking. I would walk until my feet bled if it meant that I would eventually find Aria.

I froze in mid step. There was a figure standing only a few feet from the iron gate surrounding Maria's garden and spook house. "Aria!?" I called from where my feet held me in the street. The figure did not move but I was sure it was her. It had to be. I made my feet move, one in front of the other. Then I was running to her, afraid she would step into that hideous garden.

It was the run of a dreamer. No matter how fast my feet moved or how badly my lungs screamed for more air, I couldn't seem to move fast enough. I feared for the figure ahead. When I was finally close enough so it could hear my thunderous footsteps it turned.

It was Aria! She was puzzled at why I was running. I finally reached her and put my hands on my knees, breathing hard.

"What are you doing?" she asked as if I was stupid.

"What am I doing?!" I yelled at her. "I'm coming to make sure you don't go into that garden or that awful house. What are *you* doing?"

"Thinking," she said it so simply I could hardly believe she said it. "I'm just thinking. Wait," her brow crinkled. "Why would I ever go in there?"

"I don't know, but when I saw you I thought that's what you were going to do."

"Oh, no, never. That would be suicide, Reenie. You know that." She looked off to the lonely, broken house with lonely, broken eyes. "No, I was just thinking."

"Aria . . . ?"

"Reenie, what do you think happens to people when they die?" she asked quietly.

"Aria, please don't—"

"I know you think about it too, Reenie I know you wonder if we're going to live or not," she kept her voice calm even though I was sure she would have yelled. "Answer me. What do you think happens to people when they die?"

"I suppose some go to heaven and others to Hell," I stared at her wondering when my fourteen-year-old sister started thinking such deep thoughts.

"Some stay behind don't they? Like Samuel and Maria. What if there is no after life, Reenie? What if we all just go . . . *poof.*"

"I'd like to believe that I'll see Mother and Father when my time comes."

"So do I, but it's getting hard to believe that now. How do you believe in it?" she turned to me.

I shook my head. "There has to be something else. This," I motioned around us, "can't all be for nothing. I can't let myself believe that we've gone through all of this just to pop out as if it was nothing. I just can't let myself believe that." I shook my head wondering if she would understand.

She nodded, "I'll hold onto that." She stared out over the hideous garden and that old, wretched house, and I followed her gaze. The roses looked as bad as they had in the moonlight and the sun didn't help the house's composure. No light was strong enough to make this a happy place.

I don't know what Aria saw, if she saw anything at all, but the more I stared at the old home I could see how it used to be. Right before my eyes the present version blurred and gave way to the distant past. The roses stood tall and proud, their stems a lively green. The petals changed from blood red to pink, white, yellow, and every other color I could think of. There were other flowers too. There were daffodils, sunflowers, junipers, and carnations. The grass was green and the iron gate was clean of rust.

The house was a bright white, instead of a faded brown. The doors and shutters were hinged in place and the windowpanes were whole and clear. The small chimney was all there on the roof. I saw Maria in her doorway smiling.

At first I thought she was looking at me. Then I saw the four young children playing amongst the flowers. There were three little girls and one boy. The girls laughed and giggled when their brother sneezed after sticking his nose in one of the flowers. Then, they would stick their noses in one and start sneezing too. The boy ran among the flowers chasing a stray cat. He was young and innocent. This was before he found his talent for black magic. This was when the sky was a happy blue and the clouds were puffy and white over the Lenark home. This was when the sun smiled brightly down on Maria and her four young children.

But the children started to fade away. The house began to look sickly again and the flowers started to twist in on themselves until all that was left was a sad Maria fading away from her once happy home.

Aria had left me and went back into the town. "Oh, Maria," I whispered, "I'm scared. I don't think I can do this." I stood there for a long time with my eyes closed, only feet from the iron fencing and the roses. I stood in silence, knowing that the sky wasn't as blue as it had been above Maria's head. I knew the clouds were heavier. I knew that the sun was harsh. I sighed inside. I focused on the cool breeze that played with the end of my dress. I could feel it whipping my hair about and tickling the back of my neck. It felt so good in the heat of the day.

I felt something leathery brush against my hand. It took me a moment to notice that it was real. All in a split second, I could imagine the leathery flowers reaching for me through the gate. I knew their hungry thorns were growing longer and sharper. My eyes popped open and I shrieked. I nearly fell on my butt but something steadied me.

I looked about. The roses hadn't moved a bit. That leathery thing brushed my hand again. I looked down.

Blue eyes stared up at me. "Well, hello there," I bent down next to the dog. His short fur was rough and brown. His tongue was hanging out and his mouth was set in that puppy grin. He was no puppy though. When he was on all fours his back was up to my waist. I'd never seen a dog that big before. This huge dog was gentle and friendly. Back in Mar the bigger the dog the more aggressive he was, so this surprised me greatly.

He put his paw up on my knee so I rubbed his ears. His eyes closed and his tail wagged. Then he shook his head as if he'd forgotten something. He stood up when I did. He looked up at me as if wondering where we were going. "Let's go back to town, boy," I said. He barked and his tail wiggled.

I started back to town and I expected him to run ahead of me or trail behind me like most dogs did, but no, this dog was not most dogs. He walked on my left side the entire time. This dog was so human-like I was starting to wonder if someone had turned a human into a dog.

I shook my head. "How silly is that? I was just wondering if someone had changed a human man into a dog and resulted in you." He sneezed as if to agree with me. I smiled wide and laughed. He stayed beside me the whole way to the inn but once it was in sight he barked a good-bye and ran off. "How odd . . ."

I stepped in the door and was face to face with Harro. I kept the fear from my face and walked on by him. He gently grabbed my arm and I got that slimy, dark feeling again. "What's wrong?" he asked.

"Nothing."

He raised his brows. "Renee, what's wrong? Did I do something?"

"You've done everything, Harro." I hoped his mind went to how I accused him of being rude and such. "I don't associate with men that are not *gentle*men."

He frowned, "I'm being gentle now. I'm trying to make up for everything." For a moment the slimy feeling went away, but it returned just as quickly.

"Thank you, Harro, but once someone loses my favor they don't get it back." He let go of my arm. I nodded to him and walked up those squeaky stairs.

"Renee, please, just give me a second chance. I really am trying." He followed me through the hall.

"I'm sorry but there are very few circumstances in which I give second chances. This is not one of those circumstances." I closed the door in his face. I thought Aria would have been in our room. Now that I noticed she wasn't, I felt trapped. I couldn't breathe and the room started to close in on me.

"Renee?" I took a deep breath. It had been Aria's voice that had called. "Renee, is that you?"

I leaned on the wall that separated the bedroom and the bathroom. "Yes, it's me." I could breathe now. Aria was here and we were both okay, for now at least.

She came out with wet hair. "Are you okay?" she looked me up and down. "You look a fright. What have you been doing?"

"Talking to Harro."

Aria turned to me again, her mouth gaping. I put a hand up to stop the flow of anything that she might have wanted to say. "I'm fine. He claims he wants to be a gentleman and he wants to make up for any wrong he's done me." I snorted. "As if."

"So you're okay?" I nodded in answer to Aria's question. "Don't scare me like that ever again!" She started drying her hair with a towel, looking at me sideways. "You nearly scared me half to death!"

"Excuse me if you jumped to conclusions. I'm fine, thank you very much. You would have known that if you hadn't left me at that stupid house!"

"You looked like you needed a minute, so I went off. I know how you are, Reenie. When you want to be left alone, I leave you alone; and you looked like you wanted to be left alone . . . even though you were the one to sneak up on me in the first place." She shook her head, "Never mind. I'm going to get something to eat. Are you coming?"

"No," I sat down on the edge of the bed. "I'm tired. I'll see you in the morning." Aria shrugged and left, closing the door behind her.

I took off my shoes and lay in bed for what seemed like hours. I wondered about that dog. Why was he so . . .

human-like? Maybe he really had been turned into a dog. His eyes reminded me of someone I'd met but I couldn't recall who it was. As soon as I felt the name coming to me I fell into a deep sleep.

Then and Now

I was in Maria's yard, the way it used to be. It was like the vision I'd had earlier. Maria stood and watched her children play in the sanctuary of her garden. The three little girls were wonderfully beautiful.

One was just like her mother: dark skinned with black hair and deep brown eyes. Her face was thin and stern even as she giggled. Somehow I knew her to be Eurose. It was the same way that I knew the chubby blond with brown eyes was Lubelle and that the tiny blonde with blue eyes was Tabitha. I assumed that Old Shia was blonde with blue eyes.

The three girls ran inside to their mother, carrying handfuls of flowers with them. I felt a tug on my dress and looked down to see a young, pale boy. His hair was black and sloppy; no doubt that Maria had given up trying to tame it with a comb. His innocent eyes were as black as night. As I looked down on him he shimmered. Before I knew it I was looking up at him.

He was tall enough that he kept the sun from my eyes so I could see him. The older form of the boy had the same tousled hair and dark eyes. He was lanky but powerful.

141

As he reached in his pocket for something the sky grew dull and the sun grew harsh. Maria's lovely house deteriorated to the mess it really is. The grass that was once a bright Easter-green was turning brown and dry. The beautiful flowers twisted and turned to a devastating ruby. The whole scene turned to the one at the edge of the city and I was standing in the middle of it. I looked back up to meet Samuel's eyes.

He bowed slightly and took a white rose from his pocket. He handed it to me gently and I took it nervously, afraid that if I rejected it he would grow angry. His smile grew evil and his eyes darker. I looked down to the rose in my hand.

Quickly, it was becoming leathery and cracked. Its green stem turned black and its petals bled until they were red. The thorns pricked my hands and I dropped it to the dead ground.

Samuel came closer to me, only inches away, and I backed up. I could feel the hungry thorns of the bushes behind me but that fear was nothing compared to the fear of letting Samuel touch me. I screamed when he grabbed my wrists. It wasn't just fear that made me call out; it was the pressure he was exerting on my arms. He squeezed tighter as I screamed louder. I fell to my knees in pain but he did not let go. I couldn't feel my hands any more. I could feel the roses coming around me. They closed over me as I cried out until there was nothing but blackness.

Never Alone

I felt Chene shaking my shoulders, "Renee! Renee! Wake up!" I could hear her calling to me through the blackness that they could not imagine.

Then I heard the best voice I could have imagined. "Child, come to me. Shake away the blackness." It was Kari. I struggled through the darkness and ran for her voice. "Come, child. That's right run away. Hush, now." Only then did I realize that I was still screaming. But I couldn't stop, just like I couldn't open my eyes and wake up. I started falling through the darkness and I felt Kari's bony hands grip my shoulders. "Renee! Child!" she called.

My eyes sprang open and started pouring tears. My screams turned to sobs and I couldn't even care that almost all of the people in the inn were either in my room or at my door. Through my tears I could see the red haired man and the dark haired woman. They looked odd, even in this crowd. Kari sat beside me and I buried my face in her shoulder. She rocked me and hushed me. Finally, I managed to take deep breaths and dry my eyes. I pulled away from Kari and took the tissue that Chene was holding out for me.

I looked around my room with red eyes. Not only were there people from the inn, but there were people from their houses in town. All my friends from the meetings at Kari's home were there and some I barely recognized. I closed my eyes and counted backwards from ten as Mother had taught me to do.

"Reenie?" I heard Aria whisper. "What happened?"

"It was just a bad dream," I shook my head and sniffed.

"No, Reenie, it wasn't." She took my hands, "Look." The whole room gasped so I figured that I might need to see for myself. When I opened my eyes I froze. There were bruises on my wrists. I could see a hand pattern in those dark ugly bruises. I could also see, at the end of each finger, a cut where Samuel had dug his nails into me. "Reenie?"

"Out! Everyone out!" Kari screamed, but it was only a mumble to my paralyzed ears. Jacob, Rick, and Drew nodded and started pushing the curious ones out the door. The last few people were hard to force out and started asking questions. I could feel Kari's anger and I felt a wave of power that sent those last few flying out the door. Drew locked the door behind them and sat on my bed by Aria. Rick and Jacob stood at the end of each corner of my bed and watched the door. I could hear Brandon outside yelling at the people in his quick way that probably surprised anyone out there.

"Renee, child, you must tell me what you saw. You must tell me who did this to you." I couldn't answer Kari. I could only stare at the aching contusions and bleeding cuts. Kari took my chin in her hand and forced me to look at her. She was so close that I could see white and grey streaking her hair and I could see her brown eyes misting over like the blind's. I knew she was in the line of Eurose. "Renee, answer me."

I opened my mouth, but my jaw shivered and my lips were cracked. Kari nodded so I licked my lips and tried again. "Samuel," the name came out hoarse and cracked. Jacob and Rick turned to face me now, abandoning the door.

"What happened?" Drew asked calmly.

I kept my eyes on Kari. "I was in Maria's yard, the way it used to be," I told her my story. "I saw Maria and her family. The girls went in but Samuel stayed out. He grew from a boy to a man. Everything started to go back to the way it is now: broken. Samuel gave me a white rose that turned red. He grabbed my wrists and pushed me back into those stupid flowers." I swallowed and whimpered like a child, "It hurts, Kari. It burns."

"I know, child, and we'll make it better." She turned to Jacob and Rick. "I am not strong enough after bringing her back." The boys nodded. Drew, Aria and Kari made room for each of them to sit on either side of me.

Jacob took my right hand and started to rub it gently. He mumbled strange words under his breath. It made me nervous and I wanted to pull away, but the pain started to subside.

Rick rubbed his hands together and mumbled in the same rhythm that Jacob did. Then, he gently put his hand where Samuel's had been. My wrist felt warm and fuzzy and the pain started to slip away. The bruises on both of my arms faded slightly and the cuts from Samuel's fingernails healed.

Kari's apprentices gave me my hands back and returned to their post. "Thanks." They nodded to me, feeling awkward to be in Aria's and my room.

The noise outside had faded away but I'm sure they were all waiting downstairs. It was so quiet that I was sure Chene and Barbara were giving them a good talk. Leave it to them to make someone feel guilty. I smiled at my new friends' loyalty. "Are you okay—I mean—are you *going* to be okay?" Aria asked.

"Yeah, I think so," honestly I didn't think I would be. I was afraid to go down those stairs. I was afraid to go outside. I couldn't stay in this cramp little room and, even though it was still dark out, I was terrified to go back to sleep.

I was terrified of what I would find behind my closed lids. I was terrified of Samuel reaching to me through my dreams again.

"Can I get you anything?" Drew asked.

I shook my head then, "Wait, yes. I need my robe. I need to go outside."

"No, you don't need that right now—"

"Yes, I do." I hopped out of bed. I had to see what outside looked like. Was it the same as yesterday? Had it changed like so much else had?

"No one's out there, Renee. Everyone is either here or in their own beds." Drew's comforting words was like telling a chicken to hold still when you had an ax in your hands.

"I'm not looking for a person!" I tied my robe about me and swung the door open.

Rick grabbed my elbow, "You can't go out! You need to rest. What would you see anyway? The moon?"

I spoke to Jacob, "Your vision! I have to know." I felt Rick's grip loosen and I ran down the stairs. I could hear their footsteps behind me like thunder and the talking below me like demons. I was so scared to hurdle myself into those curious eyes, into all of those questions but as I got close enough to where they could hear us coming they fell silent. Chene must have done a real number on them.

I pushed my way through the crowd, even passing Harro. I pushed by him and couldn't care if he didn't seem to like being pushed around at all. Aria, Jacob, Kari, Rick and Drew trailed behind me as if we were connected with an invisible string. I stopped short in front of the door.

Did I really want to know? Did I really want to see? Did I really want to know what was out there? Were the streets quiet and empty as Drew had promised? Were they dark and filled with red rose petals?

I placed my hand on the knob. It was trembling and shaking; it was me making it do so. I felt like I was vibrating uncontrollably. I turned the knob slowly and felt little wisps of air come through. The atmosphere was cold and heavy. It was charged with some energy. I didn't like that energy.

I opened the door.

I couldn't find the air in my lungs to scream, but many others did. I felt Aria catch me as I fell. I didn't faint but I wasn't exactly there. What had Father called it? I was having an out of body experience. Aria leaned me against the doorjamb. I felt my friends come around me as if we were attached by some sort of invisible string. I stared blankly as I heard people gasp and sob.

I couldn't make a single noise, even as I watched Harro step hesitantly into the street. He looked wary and unsure. He was Samuel's heir. He was supposed to be the one who'd done this . . . but he didn't act like it. This wasn't an act either. I could feel it rolling off of him in waves: Who did this? Who did this? Who did this? All I knew was that it wasn't Harro. Not this time.

Harro bent down and carefully picked up one evil petal. He held it between a thumb and forefinger and I watched

147

silently as it turned to dust. His face was grim as the sun crept over the horizon and the rest of the petals turned to ash, one-by-one. He backed into the inn, eyes on the road. He turned to the crowd.

"Who did this?" he called angrily. He spun about to read everyone's face. Not a soul answered. "WHO DID THIS?!" His hands balled into fists and his hair was starting to stand on end. He eyed everyone with suspicion. No, it had not been Harro. His eyes were turning blood shot and he blinked fast. He was so mad that the vibes that rolled off him smothered me. I felt like I could hardly breath, but then again I was probably hyperventilating.

I felt the darkness of unconsciousness folding in on me. I didn't want to be left alone in that darkness. Not again. I was scared but I couldn't fight it. It was too heavy and my body couldn't handle it. Rick looked at Kari meaningfully and when she nodded he ran around Harro and sat by me. Everything was turning grey. I could still see Harro shaking and trying to control his anger. He finally ran out the door. Then all that was clear was Rick's face. The crowd around us had meshed into the coming darkness. Oh, God, I was scared.

I felt Rick's hands gripping mine, "It's okay." He paused as I stared into his smooth face and his eyes. "No, I won't leave you. I'll be there with you." Had I said something? I couldn't have begged him not to let me go alone. Well, I guess I could have. His face started to fade along with everything as I tried desperately to hang on. "It's okay," Rick sounded tired now. Finally, I slipped away, only feeling Rick gripping my hands.

It was dark where I was. I was standing, maybe floating, in blackness. I whirled around. "Hello?" no one answered my call. "Hello?!" I felt like crying in that terrible silence. "No! You said you wouldn't let me be alone!"

"And I didn't," someone whispered. I turned, fearing it was Samuel. It was only Rick. "It's okay. It's just me."

I clutched my chest and tried to hear him over the pounding of my own heart in my ears. "Where are we?"

He looked around and stepped up to me. He shoved his hands in his pockets and looked all around us for a while, "We're in your head."

"How is that possible? How are you here?"

"You go here anytime you sleep . . . or faint," he looked at me. "It's just that when you sleep you fill this place with pictures—dreams. When you pass out you usually close everything out, so you never really know about this place. Since you brought me with you, you had to make a place for me to be, so we can see it." He shrugged and sat down.

"Okay," I nodded, still a little confused. "How did you get here?"

"I locked my mind with yours and hitched a ride here. You said you didn't want to be alone." He took my hands as if to remind me. "I could only imagine how frightened I would be if I had to be lost in the darkness alone after everything that has happened." He pulled me down to sit in front of him. "How are you?"

I clutched my head, "I don't know. How would you feel if you were scared to go anywhere, including your own head?"

He laughed half-heartedly. "I supposed I wouldn't be doing that great." He fiddled with a bit of leather around his neck. "Of course, I have other ways of dealing with emotions." He kept his eyes down guiltily.

"What do you mean, Rick?" he was starting to scare me. I cringed as my emotions bounced off the seamless walls of my mind and flew back to us.

"Don't be scared. It's nothing. Really." He did not meet my eyes and he played with his leather cord nervously.

"What?"

He spoke quickly, "I'm sorry. I was just worried and I couldn't just let you wonder off to Maria's house on your own. I had to keep an eye on you and Brandon agreed so—"

"Rick, what are you talking about?!"

He was quiet for such a long time that I didn't think he would answer. His feeling of shame and shyness bounced back to us, but not as strongly as mine had since this was my mind and not his. At last he looked up through thick lashes and made one single noise that made everything fall in place. That sound cleared up all his stuttering words and explained so much.

"Woof."

My jaw hung open and he smiled shyly. "You're the dog!" Everything clicked together. That dog acted so human like because in truth, he was. Those eyes in the dog's head were the same clear blue as Rick's. He looked down again and never looked up. He looked very ashamed. "Rick, it's okay. You were just looking out for me, and I'm glad you did. I just—I just can't believe . . ." No, I couldn't believe that Rick could turn into a mutt. I reached across the space between us and grabbed the string around his neck.

He looked up quickly and jumped. I didn't care that he was alarmed. I didn't care that we were closer than it was to be polite. I had to know if this was real. I could have misinterpreted the dog's attitude. I was probably imagining the color of the dog's eyes. But I couldn't have made up the feel of soft leather. That had been real.

It was true. Rick's leather cord about his neck was the same as the one around the pup's neck. It was the same thin width. It had the same texture. It was the same color, too. I rang my fingers along the little cord. I knew Rick was tense and unsure. I couldn't notice that. I could believe in magic and witches but it took a minute to absorb the new knowledge of shape shifting. I was about to reach out and touch where the cord had rubbed on skin when everything went dark and floaty.

For a moment I thought I was coming to. For a split second I thought something had gone wrong. But I could hear Rick take a deep breath and let it out slowly. I could feel his hands on my neck. Everything had gone dark because I had closed my eyes. Everything went floaty because Rick's lips had met mine.

Rick kissed me gently but there was a feeling behind it. I felt it bounce off the walls and I could identify it as desire and relief. His hands were on my neck, my shoulders, and my face. I felt warm and fuzzy. It was the best feeling I'd ever had in my entire life. I opened my eyes when I felt Rick pull away. As his lips and hands left me so did that feeling; the only thing left was a memory and a weird light headed sensation.

He backed away from me and left my gaze. "I'm sorry . . . that was out of line."

"Yes, it was," I said, but I was laughing. I couldn't help it.

"What . . . ?" Rick stared at me as if I'd lost my mind.

"You look like a scorned little puppy!" I giggled. "I'm sorry—"

Rick was laughing now too. He tried to control it but failed miserably. When we had finally settled he took my hand and kissed it. He smiled, "I'm still sorry."

I rolled my eyes, "Sure, you are." We sat there looking at each other and all around us. The darkness wasn't scary any more. It was just a quiet, serene place. "Thank you," I told Rick. "Thank you for coming with me."

I could tell he could feel everything bouncing back to us as I could; the echoes of emotions. He smiled slyly, but jokingly, and told me, "How could I risk missing the opportunity to have you all to myself?" We laughed again as it echoed over and over. It felt good to fill my lungs with joy and just breathe without worry for a few minutes. "Are you ready?"

"For what?"

"Well, it's not like we can stay here forever. I have my own mind to return to and you need to wake up," Rick reminded me.

"Oh, I can't believe I'd forgotten! This feels so unreal." I took a deep breath, "I'm ready."

Rick sat in front of me and took my hands as he had when I was swooning. "Half way through I'm going to let go," he warned me. "Don't try to hang on. Just let go. If you don't, both of us will be stuck in your body." We both cringed at that thought. "Remember to let go."

We went whirling through darkness and I felt as if I was falling. It was okay though, like that falling feeling you sometimes got before you woke up from a dream. Rick faded quickly but I could feel his hands on mine. I felt them loosening their grip and I reminded myself to let go. I kept my grip loose so he could let go when the time was right. When he did I started falling faster. It was a little nerve racking now that Rick had gone but it didn't last long. I felt a big thud in my chest and opened my eyes.

TRANSFORMATIONS

I was back in my room and lying on my bed. I sat up to see that all my friends were still with me and Rick lay beside me with his hand still on mine. "Don't take your hand off of his. He hasn't returned yet. He must journey from your body back to his." Kari looked at me from her place in a corner. She was watching Drew, Aria, Jacob, and Brandon who were watching a top spin lazily on the wood floor. It rolled to a stop and Jacob spun it again. I was about to ask how long I'd been out but Kari answered my unspoken question. "You were out just long enough for them to get bored," she smiled as a grandmother would (probably a great-grandmother in her case).

Rick sprang up, ramrod straight. He let out a deep breath and plopped back down on his back, looking around. He looked a bit disoriented, but when he looked at our hands intertwined his eyes cleared. He looked up and smiled to me.

"It's about time!" Jacob got up and stretched, followed by the others. "We thought we'd wear a whole in the floor with that old top."

"Oh, hush," Drew swatted him. "You've only been gone about fifteen minutes."

"It didn't feel like that long," Rick sat up, not letting go of my hand. "Did anything happen?"

"Not really," Brandon answered. "Harro stormed out like a mad man. I don't think he did this one, but who knows. Anyway, everyone broke out in accusations and half of them crowded around you two. We pushed 'em away and got the two of you up here, which was very hard. Rick, buddy, you weigh more than you look! Plus, we had to keep you two connected. Since then we've had to fight off white hairs and aging twenty years—"

Drew slapped him across his head. "Well, I'm happy to see that you came back okay," she told us.

I laughed, "I think Brandon was just worried."

"Was not!" he denied.

Aria smiled in triumph, "Denial is confirmation." She crossed her arms. Father had taught us that.

Kari had stood in her corner quiet as a statue. Now she spoke with true concern. "Renee, I do not think it best that you come to our meeting today. You've been through enough for one day, I think." Yes, Kari was like a mother. She was concerned and worried and watching out for me. But like most mothers she underestimated the strength and will of a child.

I shook my head stubbornly, "I'm going Kari. I need to be there more than ever now."

Kari pressed her thin lips together. She didn't like this. She didn't like this one bit. If I was her real granddaughter I knew she would force me to stay in bed all day with a watch at my door. But I wasn't hers and she had no right to do so. I was no one's to command. She nodded grimly and walked out, the others following.

I walked to the mirror in our bathroom and looked at the pale faced girl staring back. Her hair was a fright. The brown strands were tangled and frizzed. Her eyes were tired and rimmed with red. Her face was so white it could have been snow and her lips were so cracked they could have been ice. The girl licked her lips at the same time I did. She grabbed her brush and worked through her horrible hair at the same instant as I did. It was hard to believe that the ragdoll in the mirror was me.

It was even harder to believe that Maria was standing in the corner of my mirror again. She gave me the same motherly look that Kari had given me. I didn't know if she could hear me or not but I said, "I'm fine. Your son is getting on my nerves though." I wrestled out a knot and she gave me a crooked smile. Her dark eyes went to my wrists. There were little marks where Samuel's nail had dug into my flesh. The bruises could still be faintly seen. No matter how faint they were they were starting to pound again.

Maria came closer in the mirror and as she did she overcame my own reflection. I set down my brush and put my hands on the counter. I leaned towards the mirror. "Where did he get it? How could he be so evil while the rest were so good?" I referred to Samuel and her three daughters. I was afraid to say Samuel's name out loud. I was afraid that I would be calling to him. I was afraid that he would come and hurt me again. I bit my lip.

Maria didn't answer me. She just stood before me and looked at my hands. She lifted her head up quickly and smiled at me. She ducked her head back down. What was she up to? Was she thinking of a way to communicate better with me?

Her hands came towards me and I expected them to hit the other side of the glass just as mine would on this side. No, they kept reaching and her hands came out of the mirror. She grabbed my wrists. Though she held on gently I couldn't have pulled away if I had wanted to. The space in front of my eyes turned white, just as it had been so black in my head, but this was different.

I wasn't in my head; I was there in the bathroom with Maria's spirit clutching at my arms. I felt cold and icy. My blood chilled in my veins and my heart shuddered and skipped a beat. I shivered involuntarily and wondered if she was trying to kill me.

Just as quickly as the white filled my vision it subsided. Maria was gone from the mirror. My heart started working right again and my veins were flooded with warmth so fast that it burned. Why did it get so cold? Why couldn't I see?! What was Maria up too? Killing me wouldn't help her at all. It would ruin everything.

A part of me knew all these answers. I don't know if Maria was whispering them in my ear or if the part of me that had always been a witch knew. Somehow I just knew these answers, but they didn't make me feel any better.

I had been cold. Maria had touched me. Maria was dead so she was cold. It wasn't as if she'd touched me in a dream and I could imagine that it wasn't that way. She was dead and cold and that was that.

The blank whiteness that had imprisoned me was Maria's world. She wasn't here on earth with us but she wasn't in the afterlife either. When she chose to stay behind she got caught between the worlds of the living and the dead. She had been cast away to a place that was undefined; it was a place that was never meant to exist.

People weren't meant to stay behind.

I looked down at where Maria's hands had been, exactly where Samuel's had been. I gasped in shock. There was just smooth skin to be seen. There were no marks to indicate that Samuel had ever harmed me. There wasn't a throbbing pain in my veins either. She had healed me the rest of the way. She hadn't been trying to kill me even though I felt a bit of death when she touched me. She wasn't ruining everything. She was just helping. She was just being the mother that she had always been.

I smiled and thanked her silently. I just hoped that no one would notice. It would be too hard to explain to them that Maria had really come to me again and that she had really healed me. It would be too hard to explain that I felt the world in which Maria was trapped; I had felt death. I couldn't explain that and I wasn't going to explain to any other noisy people why she had done it. I wasn't going to review my unexpected meeting with Samuel.

After I had finished with my hair I headed down stairs. "Renee," Barbara called me over to the bar. "Here, this is on the house." She pushed a plate to me. It was a chocolate piece of cake with ice cream in the middle. "It's my comfort food when I'm upset so maybe it will help you out." She held up her hand and continued with her strange accent, "No, don't thank me. You need it."

"Thanks," I said anyway. I smiled and took a bite of the cake. It was really good and when Barbara noticed that I thought so she smiled proudly and pranced to the back of the kitchen.

There weren't many people in the inn today. I would imagine that most of the people were at home with their families now. None of my friends were there and I didn't see Chene wondering about in the kitchen. When Barbara passed I asked, "Where is everyone?"

She knew what I meant. Her eyes skimmed the room and she whispered, "At Kari's." She kept on her job in the kitchen I ran out the door and hurried to Kari's. When I slid through the door everyone was sitting down and Kari and Rick were standing up. I sat by Aria as everyone settled. "Why didn't you get me?"

"I didn't want to stress you out." She said simply. I was about to say something back when Kari spoke.

"Hush. Hush," she tried in her usual patient voice but the people kept on with their whispering. She frowned. "Shut up!" I jumped back, as everyone else had, and stared at her. "I will not tolerate it today!" she looked about the room. "The time is near—I feel it in these old bones! I have two lessons for you today. One is extremely difficult and the other even more so. First you will communicate with your minds."

Rick sat down and Wanda stood up. I assumed that the lesson plan had changed. "Wanda, tell Gretchen what you are going to think. Whisper it in her ear." Wanda leaned down and whispered in a small blond girl's ear.

"Good," Kari kept on. "Now, Wanda, think of that same thing. Think of it clearly in your head. Make sure it's loud and clear." Kari nodded. "Gretchen, Wanda was going to think of a picture, am I right?" The young girl nodded. "Was it of a duck in a pond?"

Gretchen nodded in awe.

"It looks easy but I am old and I have had many years to master it. Begin!" I could tell Kari was running on a short fuse today. She must have been shaken more than anyone by the news of my dream and the red roses.

I turned to Aria. "You first," I said. I listened hard for her thought. I opened up my mind, but all that did was make Kari's clock tick louder. I listened for what felt like hours but wasn't that long, I was sure. I didn't dare break my concentration to look for the time. Then I heard a rhythm.

It was only three syllables. Whatever Aria was thinking, it was high pitched and taunting. I listened harder and tried to separate and clarify the thought. I rolled my eyes and motioned that it was my turn.

I thought my answering thought loud and clear. I thought it over and over again: *Yes, I like Rick. Yes, I like Rick.* Aria listened for a long time too. Eventually she cocked her ear to me and leaned in as if that would help. When she finally heard it she bounced up and down and held back giggles. She mouthed, "I knew it," to me. She clasped her hands over her mouth to keep from disturbing the others around us.

We went back and forth like this forever but the clock hands moved slowly. Aria got bored with our usual banter so she turned to Meagan, leaving me to think. Rick was across the room communicating with Brandon and Jacob. He was fingering that little leather cord about his neck again. Jacob and Brandon looked at him seriously. Whatever they were discussing it was making him nervous. He just kept fidgeting with the cord faster and faster.

I was about to try listening in on their conversation when I heard another voice in my head. *Hello.*

Rick? I thought. No, I knew that wasn't Rick. He wasn't talking to me right now. This voice was too strange. It was husky and deep. I looked around for anyone who might've said something to me. It didn't look like anyone had.

No, guess again. I'll give you three hints, the voice came again. *Who do you hate most? Who frightens you the most? Who's hurt you most?*

Harro? The thought of him getting into my head was absolutely terrifying and I felt my stomach flop with unease.

Close, the voice mocked.

Samuel, I thought with conviction. It had to be him.

You're a smart girl, Renee. If you were really smart you would make a deal with me, Samuel taunted me. *If you were smart you would stop helping my mother and that little group of yours. I might let you die quickly in the end. Who knows, I might even let you live.*

I know that's not true. You want me dead more than anyone.

Not true! I would like my mother to be officially dead, but other than her, yes. You are *a smart girl. So I won't let you live. I can make it quick though. Just stop with your little hero trick.* His voice lingered in my mind like the smell of a dead animal did long after it had deteriorated.

I thought to myself for a while. Why is he doing this? *The only reason you'd be making this deal is because you're afraid it might work. You're afraid that we might pull it off.*

The voice was quiet.

Well, your plan just back fired, Samuel. I know you're not completely confident. I'm going to work even harder now. I will *win.* I was confident. If Samuel was afraid that meant we might have a chance.

I heard his disgusting laughter ring through my head. *You are wrong, Renee. Your plan just backfired! You will die slowly!* he screamed in my head. I knew he was gone. I felt a part of my head go empty for a second then return to normal. The split second of emptiness felt good; Samuel's voice had felt slimy on my thoughts.

I looked at Kari who was hovering over Meagan and Aria. *Kari?* I called for her attention in my head. She looked down at me and I replayed the memory of what had happened, knowing that I couldn't keep something like this from her. She didn't say a word. She didn't think a word. She remained utterly silent as I replayed the whole thing in my head and sent it to her. At the end she just nodded. As she walked away from me I noticed that many people had been watching us. They dodged their heads down quickly and I wondered how many had been listening in.

She walked toward Rick and nodded. He stood up smiling and ready for something. As he stood he winked at me and I couldn't help but smile.

Kari interrupted my moment. "Do your heads hurt?" she asked us. We all nodded, some of us winced. "Well, they're about to hurt more. Shape shifting is extremely difficult. I would show you myself but my old body cannot handle it anymore." She stepped back and waved for Rick to do his part.

Rick stepped into the ring of people and took a deep breath. He looked at me a bit shyly and then transformed.

His body seemed to fold in on itself and collapse inside. He became smaller and smaller and fur replaced clothing. He came down on all fours. It happened so fast and smoothly that I could hardly believe it happened.

Meagan laughed and smiled, "Does he do tricks?"

Rick, in his dog form, growled and bore his teeth. The fur on his back stood up making him look like a wolverine. I was afraid he was going to jump her, but he didn't. As soon as Meagan had reared back in surprise and fright he sat down on his haunches. He did that dog smile with his tongue hanging lopsided out of his mouth. His blue eyes traveled over the crowd.

Kari spoke up, "It takes hard work for someone to transform like that; thank you, Rick." Rick looked up and barked. "For some people this is very hard to do. For all you people in here that may be descendants of Eurose, as I am, I can tell you that it is not easy at all. Eurose was never that good at shape shifting. However," she turned to Aria and me, "those who are descendants of Lubelle are in for a treat. Lubelle took well to this. Before she died she had mastered half a dozen forms." She smiled at us.

"Just work hard and try your best. Some of you will never shape shift, but that's just how it works sometimes." She sat down in a chair and watched all of us have our go.

"Oh my Gosh! Renee, what do you suppose I'll be?" Aria's face was flushed with excitement and I had to laugh at her.

"Whatever animal you hold in mind," Rick stood by us in his human form. "Just imagine an animal and try to compact your body into it; but don't imagine anything like a duck, that won't do you any good. Try to imagine something that can do things. A dog can go places without being noticed. They can do all sorts of things."

"What kind of dog was that supposed to be anyway? I've never seen anything like it," I questioned.

"It was a coyote."

I nodded. They didn't have those in Mar.

Aria was practically shaking with joy. All of a sudden she got really still and closed her eyes. She must have figured out what animal she wanted to be. I prayed that she didn't imagine an elephant. It would be just like Aria to imagine a big pink elephant.

Rick left us to help others that were starting to get frustrated already. I thought for a moment by my immobile sister. I wanted to be something beautiful and powerful. I thought of an owl, but what good would an owl do? I thought of one of the big jungle cats Father had told me about. He said he'd encountered a huge black cat once; he'd called it a panther. No, that was too noticeable. I looked over to Rick and smiled. I knew what I would be.

I closed my eyes and imagined my animal. I stood there motionlessly until my feet hurt, but I stayed like that. I calmed down and took deep, steady breaths. I found my mind was silent was clear, though my legs were a little numb from standing there so long.

I felt the hair on my neck bristle with a breeze that wasn't there. My fingernails hurt and my head pounded, but I kept the animal in my mind and held still. My teeth hurt and my feet hurt. Even my tailbone hurt! As soon as I thought my head would explode it stopped. Everything was quiet.

Then the room burst out in clapping. I opened my eyes and flinched. Everything was so clear, it was almost disorienting. Everything was so sharp in the sense of a husky.

Every winter the dog sled teams went through Mar for a pit stop. I'd seen all the dogs, but the huskies were the most beautiful of all. The way they pulled the sled and their owner they must be strong and smart too.

"It might take a little getting used to," Rick called from across the room. I barked at him.

Kari motioned me into the hall. There was a huge mirror in her bathroom. In the reflection there was me, and about a dozen people that had followed. At first I wasn't sure about it. I cocked my head to the left and to the right and the dog in the mirror did the same thing. It was me! I barked cheerfully and wagged my curled tail.

A cat came up beside me. *How weird is that? I choose to be a cat and you choose to be a dog!* I heard the thought in my head. Aria sat in front of me as a black cat, her tail swishing lazily.

Over the course of Kari's lesson I went back and forth to my different forms of human and animal as more joined in. Kari's house was turning into a zoo of disciplined creatures.

There were dogs and cats; falcons and rabbits. I wondered what a rabbit was good for but then I remembered how fast they were.

When we all departed I was happy for once. It felt good to be able to have a private conversation with someone—completely private. And being an animal had felt amazing. Everything I did was easier because of the instinct. I could see better and hear better and smell better. But Rick had been right: the new vision takes a while to get used to.

Chene even took off a little longer to have dinner with us. None of us talked out loud for fear that Harro would be listening in. I don't know why it would have mattered. We mainly talked about our lives.

We told Chene what it was like in Mar and she told us what it was like in Roe when she was a kid. We talked about our choice of animal and I had to explain mine all over again.

Not many people want to pass a black cat's path, Aria thought to us. *Plus, I can scratch and bite and run fast. I can fit in small spaces and if I fall off of anything I'll just land on my feet.*

Chene had been the rabbit. *I've never been much of a fighter. Being a rabbit suits me. Since I can run so fast I can be more of a messenger, bringing news back and forth and such.*

We made fun of some of our friend's choices. The girl that Kari called Gretchen had chosen to be and owl. Chene told us that she's absolutely terrified of heights. We laughed at the remembrance of Jacob being a Rottweiler. It suited him perfectly; it was just a funny picture. He had sat on his haunches sitting tall. It was typical Jacob.

We were about to go our separate ways when there was a scream from out in the streets. It was a horrible shriek, one

164

that would reach the heavens. There was light outside when it was supposed to be dark. I ran to the door and swung it open wide. I heard everyone in the inn follow behind me as I stepped into the road.

THE HUMAN THREAT

The market was burning high and bright. People were screaming at the man who was still pouring liquid on the carts. He stood so tall in his trench coat, as if what he was doing was perfectly reasonable. His red hair was the color of the flames, his eyes black in the shadows.

He threw the can of liquid down as his friend came up. Her smile was as dark as her hair—evil and unappealing. She handed him a weapon, holding her own in the mayhem. Already people were flooding the street, taming the flames with their magic, others with buckets of water. But the two did not seem to mind. They raised their weapons: crossbows. My uncle had used them to hunt wild creatures; the arrows were crude and terrifying.

I looked about.

They weren't planning on burning a city of witches. The fire was just the bait and we were just moths to the flame, waiting to be killed. The perfect prey. But no one else could see it. They were helping the burned and wounded. They were getting the fire under control and trying to decide how to approach the offenders. How could they approach them? They looked crazy: no fear, just laughing.

They raised their weapons and shot. Both of them found a target and screams filled the sky and bounced off the distant mountains. In the distance livestock were panicking and more people, like fools, came out of their houses. Some stepped back in fear and shock. Some stepped forward trying to use their magic to bind them. But nothing would work.

The man laughed and the two held out small bags tied around their necks. "We know your ways, devils! Your evil cannot touch us!" Chene took a step closer, attempting to sneak up to the girl. "May," the man nodded to the dark haired girl. She pulled the trigger of her crossbow. But I used my power, not to stop her, but to push Chene out of the way.

The man turned to me, infuriated. "Ricardo," the woman spoke to him, "we must kill them all." And Ricardo pulled his own trigger.

I cringed, covering my head with one arm and putting out the other. After a moment the arrow should have hit me . . . and when it did not I opened my eyes. The arrow stood frozen in front of me, just in front of my hand. I smiled but in a rage the intruders started shooting their arrows in the dimming light of the fire. "Devil worshippers!" they accused us.

Chaos. The magic weavers were intimidated by two humans . . . because it meant others may grow brave enough to come.

I pulled Aria into a doorway, "Stay here!" I ran back out to help my friends, some of who were on the ground now. We tried endlessly to affect them but whatever was in those bags kept them protected. And at last the fire diminished, leaving us in the dark. Anywhere they aimed would be okay. But if we did so blindly, we would harm our own.

I was so afraid in the dark, unable to see anything. People shrieked around me and I hear thuds as some fell. It was like being in one of my dreams and I could not escape.

Shaking, I got on my hands and knees, hoping I'd be less of a target.

Footsteps in the distance sent a shiver down my spine. They were heavy and determined. *Oh, God,* I thought. *I'm going to die!* They stopped just behind me. I heard someone breathing angrily. "Fools," a voice muttered and the half demolished market went up in flames again. The light hurt my eyes but I opened my eyes to see who was there.

Harro, looking very fatal, stood near me. He walked forward, deflecting arrows. "You have no right to be here. This is my city and you are just rats, needing to be exterminated." His teeth were bared and his jaw was taut. I feared he would grow fangs and horns but he just kept on.

The crossbow was so close to his chest now and I found myself confused. I wanted Harro to kill Ricardo. I wanted Ricardo to kill Harro. I watched as Chene finally tackled the girl, May, and as her weapon went flying.

Harro grabbed the crossbow at his chest and pulled it aggressively. Ricardo's shoulder popped and he let out a curse I couldn't help but cringe at. The man swung at Harro but his attack was easily dodged. In his momentum, Ricardo passed his opponent. As he did, Harro grabbed the back of the man's neck, bending him backwards. "Are there any others?"

Ricardo grinned, teeth chipped and brown. "You will burn on judgment day." He laughed a guttural sound.

As Harro pulled out a knife he whispered, "You'd have to figure out how to kill me first." The blade glinted before he drove it under the man's chin. Harro let him drop to the ground to choke on his own blood and suffocate to death.

People were going back to their houses now and helping those who were hit. Some were still in a panic, but I could not do anything but watch Harro. He walked over to where Barbara was helping her mother restrain the last threat.

May spit at him, "You cannot touch me, demon!"

He cocked his head and looked at her smiling. "That pouch around your neck only protects you from magic. It doesn't mean I can't touch you," he ran the back of his hand down her cheek. "Are there any more of you?"

"I will never tell you!"

"You will," he frowned. "I'm losing my patience. Are there any more of you?" His eyes burned in the firelight.

"Bastard!" she spat in his face. I could tell she had just pushed him too far. Because, in truth, he was a bastard.

He closed his fist around her tiny throat, dangling her from the ground. Chene and Barbara back away, too close to Harro for comfort. "Tell me." May struggled and cursed him. A small blade protruded from the toe of her boot and she swung her leg to him. He caught it in one large hand.

"Tell me," his voice was just as calm and deliberate as before. She thrashed against his grasp when Harro squeezed her ankle. I heard bone crush and I choked back bile as she shrieked.

Tears streaked down her cheeks. "No! No! It was only us! There is no one else!" She sobbed the words out.

"Good," Harro dropped her and she clutched her ankle, writhing on the ground. As he waltzed away he picked up her own weapon and shot her with it. The arrow stuck between her open eyes, blood running into them. He walked in to the darkness as the light of the fire began to dim once again.

"Renee?!" I looked up to see Rick calling for me in the clutter of people. When he spotted me he ran to me, kneeling. "Are you okay?" When I nodded he helped me to my feet and into the inn.

People were everywhere being tended to. The worst were laid on tables and the bar; the others sat in chairs and on the floor, clutching at their injuries. "How many are . . . are gone?" I mustered up the courage to ask.

Rick bit his lip. "Many are hurt, but they will live. However . . . three did not make it. Gretchen—from our meetings—was the first hit. Kale and Raven, who you didn't know, will be buried tomorrow, as well."

My breath left me. Three more claimed. How many more were going to die while I was here? "I have to help them," I tried to pull away to help those who were crying and gritting their teeth in pain.

"Renee," Rick reasoned with me as he lead me up the stairs, "you are too weak and in shock. You've been through too much today." He opened my room door and I looked around for Aria. "Your sister is perfectly fine. Barbara and Drew are trying to coax her out of the kitchen closet. She just spooked a little." He sat me on the bed. "Now rest."

I stood, "No, I need to help Aria and the others." I felt sick to my stomach with the violence and wanted to fix some of it. Though I was exhausted I had to do something. I was tired of being useless.

Rick's hand paused on the doorknob. His face looked strained when he told me, "Renee, please don't make me do this." I rolled my eyes, having no idea what he was talking about, and went to go to the door. He frowned and waved his hand in front of my face, "Sleep."

I collapsed and Rick caught me. The last thing I remember was trying to push him away and stand back up.

BRIEFLY

The next days were filled with sadness and determined training. And occasionally Aria and I were forced to stay in our rom to rest. Little did they know we practiced there, as well.

The little town was growing melancholy. I could feel the despair over me like a wet blanket. But we all kept on. And no one had seen Harro since that fiery night. It was suspected that he went off to the dark of the mountains to brew but no one knew for sure.

"'Morning, Barbara," we had stopped saying "good" in front of our greeting. She nodded and slid a plate of eggs and sausage towards Aria and me. We ate slowly in the silence of the inn. People seemed too scared to talk, too stressed to waste that energy. I felt the same. We all spooked and our hearts skipped a beat when the door opened and Harro walked in. He ignored us as he put on his stained apron and took a stack of plates from a frozen Chene to take to the back and wash. It seemed that even he desired some normality.

That night made a week that nothing had happened. Rick was walking me back from dinner and we managed to laugh a little. The stars had finally revealed themselves, the clouds rolling out over the sea. We were still on the outskirts of town, opposite from Maria's house, when he stopped me to look up to the sky.

"I'm sorry all of this is happening," he sighed.

"It's not your fault. The man and woman last week were unpredictable. And what has happened concerning Maria and . . . her son," I could not say his name, "would have happened no matter when I came."

"I know," he took my hand. "I wish you weren't our savior. Sometimes." I looked at him. "I mean—it's just—" he rubbed his head. "I mean, if you weren't destined to fight all of this you could have a normal time here."

"Normal? Here?" I laughed. "I can't imagine that!"

"At least we could . . ." he laughed at himself and the words coming out of his mouth. "It would be normal."

I looked at him. "Come now, Rick. You're starting to talk like Kari! I can't understand you."

He looked at me finally. He looked so tired, almost broken. He wrapped his arms around me easily and put his forehead to mine. I stood there nervously in contrast to his calm. This was breaking all the rules. As it was, we shouldn't have been out alone together. Especially not like this.

He placed a hand on my cheek and kissed me as if it was nothing new . . . and I did not stop him. He pulled away to look at me. "This wouldn't have to be so complicated." His meaning was clear and I put my head against his shoulder suddenly very tired, too.

"Maybe after all of this is over we could restart," I suggested.

"I'd like that," I could hear him smiling. But he pulled away suddenly.

I felt ridiculous. "What's wrong? Did I say something?" I followed his line of sight when he did not answer me. A glow was rising in the distance, soft and yellow but growing. Panic filled me. "Aria!" I raced off, Rick following instantly.

When we reached the fire we could see it was leading straight to the inn. We ran through the pastures, causing horses to run and cows to pause in their grazing. At last we cut through an ally near the inn. People were spilling into the streets and as soon as I spotted Aria I ran to her.

"I'm fine, Renee. Just get ready," she told me. I looked back to the flames.

Houses were burning and people ran through the streets. One woman was having water poured on her to get the fire out. The light of the fire hid the stars and smoke replaced the sky. And coming from the fire and smoke was a demon. His hair was orange in the fire and his eyes were a color I've never seen. He was glorious in the sparks and his evil smile was beautiful.

Harro was doing this. Harro was burning away all evidence of Roe. He walked by Kari's burning house and what remained of the market. As he walked by the library it smoked and trembled and flames licked up its sides. People ran from him in fear and disgust.

Brave ones assembled behind my sister and me. I felt Jacob shivering with anger and I felt Drew's calm, grave acceptance of all of this horror. But even the brave ones flinched and gasped when two more figures came out to stand beside Harro. Drew screamed in anger and Rick had to hold her back.

Must Be Strong

"Traitor!" she screamed. "Bastard!" She tried to break free from Rick's hold. Drew kicked and threw her weight about, but Rick kept his arms around her until she stopped moving and he was sure she wouldn't charge off to kill her twin.

Meagan walked next to Harro proudly. She wore a black dress that matched Harro. Behind her she left red rose petals that were consumed in the fire. I knew then that Meagan had spread the petals that morning. I knew then that my instinct about her had been right. Meagan was dark and wrong. Her face was distorted in anger and her hands were in fists at her sides. She smiled vilely at Drew.

Drew closed her eyes to keep the tears of betrayal in and to control her growing rage. She clenched her fists until I saw her hands bleeding. I didn't stop her, though. If I did I knew she would lose it.

I looked back to the trio in black and finally let my eyes rest on the one I knew was Samuel. He was there but see-through. He was a dark angel in all black like the others, but even more so. His black hair framed his face like a mad man and his eyes were pits of beasts and monsters. He was walking straight for us, gliding over the stones with every step, only like a spirit could. Even though he was dead, even though he had to feed off of his son's power, I feared him the most.

He held out his hand as he walked and Chene screamed. She twitched in unbearable pain. This was it, this was the first attack. This was black magic at work.

This was war.

The part of me that always knew I was a witch grew hot and sparked and took over. I set my eyes on Samuel and screamed with the pain that I'd let build up and simmer. He bent forward as if he had just been hit in the gut then flew back into the fire, releasing Chene. Drew was shaking beside me; all of the emotion was out of her eyes . . . all but one. She wanted to kill. I could see it in her grey eyes; I could see her bloodlust.

"Now," I told her.

I felt something inside of my friend snap like a rubber band stretched too far and I could feel the waves of power move around me as her hair rose. I could feel her push her power at an amazing speed to her sister.

Meagan's scream joined those around us. She gripped her ears and tore at her hair. She cringed on the ground. I could only imagine what Drew was putting in her head; I didn't even want to imagine such things. Meagan fell to the ground breathing deeply, but she had stopped her yelling.

"I'm not letting you die that easily," Drew whispered. I'd always known that my friend had been powerful beyond my belief but only now did I see the true extent of what she could do and what she *would* do.

The crowd behind me spread across the street to form a frightened line, a line that we could not let our foes cross. I felt them shoot waves of power to our enemies and I saw Harro and Meagan block most of them. They were so powerful. Some in my line fell around me and got back up . . . some didn't, whether they were dead or not. Everyone from my lessons at Kari's was there. But there were many faces that I did not know and more were joining us.

Aria stood at my side as we fought. Flames were around us and I felt a sheen of sweat on my skin. None of it mattered to our enemies as they slowly approached us and as Samuel burst forth from the smoke and rejoined his troop.

Aria fell beside me as she moaned. Samuel kept his eyes on her, torturing her in a way that I wouldn't have wished on my worst enemy . . . until now. My sister lay at my feet. I felt something break inside of me. I saw every wrong the world had done me. I held it in my mind, letting it burn. I saw Father dead all over again. I heard the cheers of the people watching my mother burn. I saw the life go out of her eyes again. I relived our ride from Mar to Roe. I remembered the pain Harro and Samuel had caused me since I'd arrived. I saw Luke's body in my mind, mangled and pitiful, and poor Gretchen's tombstone.

Now I saw the fire around me. I saw the trio of dark witches coming on us.

I saw my sister at my feet, moaning and trying to breathe.

The last thing I had snapped and with it everything sucked in towards me. The wind made everyone lean towards me. The flames pointed to me and smoke and bits of rubble flew to my feet. In that one moment it was silent and the pressure of the air was so heavy many fell to their knees.

Then I let it all go. I directed all of my hurt and anger and pain to those three advancing figures. The energy flew to them, tearing stones off the road and shaking the ground with it. The wind blew out a line of fire and cast people up against their houses. When it hit the trio I felt . . . good. It hit them with such force that they collapsed to the ground and flew back.

As they lay there I approached them, even though I knew they were not dead. The others followed with me. We continued on even as Harro got to his feet, then Samuel, then Meagan. I was proud of the scrapes that covered them at random. I was proud that some of the stones that had gone flying had hit them. It felt good to see Harro and Meagan bleed. It was surprising to see that Samuel could too, but I got over the surprise soon enough.

Meagan set off a wave that was strong enough to make my group slide back a few feet.

As the flames grew again waves were going through the streets. It was a battle of power. Our waves and shocks of magic were like arrows moving across the battlefield. They soon became swords as the trio moved into our ranks. With a touch we could put each other to our knees. More of my friends fell, but this time I knew some of them were dead. I knew they'd gone somewhere else to watch this mess.

I knew the dark ones were feeding off of the town's panic and fear. So I fed off of anger. I let the anger of others flow into me. I let myself feel their pain and that made me stronger.

Even as we were being pushed further across town, further to Maria's house, I grew stronger. I knew I should have been getting tired, mentally and physically, but I wasn't. I felt the adrenaline burn in my veins as I was pushed back.

I shrieked when Harro touched me. His hand gripped my shoulder from behind. The pain was like nothing I'd ever felt. It took over my nerves and I couldn't think. I couldn't push him away. When I fell he kept his hand on me, no doubt using the other to block others from helping me. Hot tears spilt from my eyes. I felt like I was burning from the inside out. I turned my head and bit his arm as hard as I could. I heard him scream and when he pulled away I spat blood from my mouth.

But it hadn't been my little bite that had made him cry out. Rick stood behind Harro hitting him with a piece of wood that had fallen from a house. Harro turned quickly and blasted Rick into the crowd. When he turned to me I was ready. I placed my hand on his chest and he bellowed in pain. I blew him into a house and turned to keep fighting as a warrior turns from one foe to the next.

We were so close to Maria's house now. We were losing.

I saw Meagan on top of her twin, trying to choke Drew. I shifted without really knowing it. In my dog form I pounced on Meagan and threw her off. I sunk my sharp teeth into her calf. She kicked me away but I jumped on again. She threw me off and ran into the crowd to attack someone else. I spat skin out of my mouth. I looked up to see Drew smile at me in two ways.

That smile thanked me for saving her life.

That smile also acknowledged my idea. She shifted into a hawk and flew off.

I soon found out that I could work magic in my dog form, not just when human. Samuel grabbed me by the scruff of the neck. As I whimpered I knew the pain wasn't as bad. I could handle it in this form; I could think. I shot him away as he screamed. Hearing that scream made everything just a little bit brighter.

A few yards away I could see Rick fighting Harro and no one could help. I ran towards them on all fours. I bounced off of Jacob who was trying to stand up and flew into Harro's face. My claws dug into his shoulders and my teeth aimed for his neck. He moved enough so I only caught the edge of his jaw. No matter where I could sink into I would hold on. And I did as Harro screamed and swatted at me. I felt my teeth sink through flesh and muscle. When I hit bone I was finally thrown off.

As Harro stood and started to me I dashed between people's legs and escaped. I stopped on the edge of the crowd and changed back. I looked over the fight. Frightened people had ventured into it and my dear warriors had to fight them off too. I shook my head. What a mess.

I whipped around at the sound of a yell and was hit with a tremendous amount of magic. Meagan was on top of me, trying to hit me. I hit her in the nose and stood up. I held my ribs. They were aching from the damage she'd caused. She came to rush on me and I was ready for her . . . until she cheated. She pulled out a small knife. I tried to move but she slashed my arm.

She ran to me again and I knew she would kill me. But she stopped and choked out a small scream. A bit of slivered wood stuck through the front of her gut. She dropped to the stone street to reveal Drew. She had stabbed her own sister for me. She'd killed her own sister to save me . . .

Meagan looked up and gurgled, "Sister?" through a mouth full of blood.

Drew looked down on her through misty eyes, "You are no sister of mine." She walked away trembling and left me to watch her sister die.

This was insane! This fight was killing people and separating families. This battle was burning away an entire town. But this was war. This was how it was.

I left Meagan's body where it lay and ran back into the crowd. Jacob had shifted too and tore at Samuel with everything he had. Every time he was forced off he sprang back with bared teeth. I shifted and joined him. Together we pulled Samuel to the ground. It was strange to tear at something that could be seen through. He threw us off one last time and ran into the crowd like a coward.

Over the crowd I could see Aria as a cat slashing away at Harro's face. She was latched onto the back off his head and reached around to take another swipe. Harro managed to grab her and throw her into the scurry of people. I watched as she landed on her feet and returned to her post. She bit his ear and he screamed. He threw her off again but she took a chunk of him with her.

I saw Drew swipe down as a hawk and try to tear at his eyes. She didn't get to but Harro fell back onto the stones of the road. I saw a snake wrap its thick body around his neck. Brandon was in on the game too. He bit into the hand that was trying to unravel him. Those long fangs sank deep and ripped at the flesh when Harro tried to pull away.

I smiled and wagged my tail.

A man was swinging an iron rod in a circle and hitting anyone he could. My friends were trying to contain him but they couldn't. The man swung about crazily screaming, "No! Don't touch me! I'll kill you! No!" He held onto the rod with both hands and continued to spin around. He was old and probably couldn't tell friend from foe anymore.

In my low plain I ran under him and latched onto his hands. He screamed in horror and fell back, releasing the rod. I barked at him fiercely and he started to reach for his weapon. I laid my ears back and showed my teeth. The hair on my back rose. I barked over and over as he scooted his way out of the crowd and into a doorway.

I yelped as someone stomped on my foot. I twirled to see who it had been but I saw something else. Samuel blew away all of my friends and freed his son. Together they tried to blast away everyone who came on them. Drew circled in the air above them unnoticed. I watched as she swooped down and finally took one of Harro's eyes. She managed to do what no else could. She separated the duet of demons.

Harro went running and holding his face. I saw him go down in an excited frenzy of animals and people. I was about to laugh as a fox sprang high into the air and joined the pile when I caught Samuel out of the corner of my eyes.

He swooped down and grabbed a black kitten. He took off through the crowd with my sister, blocking off every force of magic and dodging all the people that threw themselves at him.

My mind went red. Samuel had my sister and was running for his old house. Samuel was going to take my little sister there, to that evil place where darkness grew freely and untamed. I ran after him, dodging between legs and jumping over fallen friends while one thought repeated itself in my head.

Kill.

Kill.

Kill.

I ran into the darkness without hesitation.

A part of me knew that this was just Samuel's trap. He was just luring me in to kill me. With no one else around, no one could save me; no one could help me. He wanted this. He wanted to kill me slowly. He said he would. I had never been one to rely that much on promises and I knew this one would be broken too. Samuel had been waiting too long for this to kill me slowly. But I knew it would hurt.

I knew that the chances of me defeating him were slim to none. I knew this was exactly what Samuel wanted.

But that was just a part of me. The rest of me only knew that a demon had my little sister. I knew he was going to hurt her and I knew I couldn't let him do that. I had promised her that it would all be okay. I would try to keep this one promise with everything I had. I knew that I had to do this. This wasn't a matter of waiting to get people to help or thinking it over. This wasn't a matter of "I can't" or "I won't". I had to. I had no choice in this. My little sister was in the hands of the worst person I'd ever known.

I jumped the rusty old iron fence. In doing so I crossed a very fragile line. Even if I wanted to I couldn't go back now. This was it. I raced through the rose bushes. I felt their thorns try to tear at me but my fur was too thick for that. I felt their sickly stems brush against me as I plowed through. I felt their leathery petals, but I didn't care. I barely knew any of this as I followed the scent to where Aria would be, to where Samuel would be.

I pushed my way through the tangles of disgusting, half-dead flowers. At last I burst through to where the ground was clear to stand in front of the door of Maria's house. The dead grass crunched under my feet and the smell of smoke still reached me out here where the sky was dark and the air was cool.

Samuel stood in front of me clutching Aria's arm. He stood smiling at me in triumph. I'd taken the bait just as he knew I would.

Aria stood next to him, prisoner. She was in her human form now and she was having trouble controlling the fear. She was as still as a statue and probably as cold as one. Her lips were pressed into a thin line and her jaw was taut. Her eyes shimmered with tears in the moonlight. She shook her head at me, disappointed because I was too stupid to just let her die here. I had to go die with her.

"I thought you were smart, Renee. How disappointing," Samuel mocked me. His voice was deep and husky just like when he had gotten into my head. "But it's much easier this way." He squeezed Aria's arm again. She gave him nothing but a whimper.

The fur on my back rose and tingled. My ears were so far back on my head they might have been glued. I showed my teeth and clenched them until they hurt. My nails dug into the dead earth and I trembled with rage as many people's blood dripped from my teeth with a metallic taste.

I set one foot forward.

"No," he said.

I growled.

"No," he squeezed Aria again. This time it was with his mind. She choked back a scream and crinkled in on herself.

I put my foot back and watched Aria regain her composure.

She was so pale and frail looking. I'd never seen my sister look so strong. I'd never seen her fight so hard. Not when we watched our mother die, not when we were on the ship, not even when she had torn off part of Harro's ear. That had all been easy. Now she stood in the hands of Samuel Lenark. She gave him nothing. My little sister, only fourteen years of age, was being stronger that I ever could have been.

Aria did not cry. She did not scream. She did not yell or beg or plead. She took her punishment that she did not deserve with pride. Even as she shook and tried for air and got paler with every second she was beautiful. She was an angel. She gave me strength.

"Why don't you change into you're true form, Renee?"

I did so before he could hurt my angel again. I stood there quietly. Blood dripped from my arm and I heard the bushes behind me rustle.

"That's better—"

"You bastard! You traitor! Murderer!" I screamed. I had no idea where it had come from. I hadn't thought about saying that. I knew it could get Aria and I both killed. I shook violently. It was much easier in my husky form to retain my emotions.

Samuel shook his head as if I was a child that had just repeated a bad word. Aria screamed and clutched her ears. She bit her lip to stop the screaming but she still moaned. Samuel let her fall to his feet. She looked at me blankly. She was as white as the moon and the blood from the spilt in her lip looked black in the silver light. I couldn't tell what she was trying to tell me from her face but I heard her words in my head.

"Just go. Leave here before he takes you too."

But I couldn't leave. I wouldn't leave her to die, scared and alone. I'd already crossed that line. Even if I tried to leave I knew Samuel would kill me in mid step. I thought all of this.

Aria dropped her head to the dirt. She knew I was right. She had to know.

FEAR AND FAITH

"I wouldn't do that again," Samuel warned. He was completely unaware of everything we'd just conversed. "I told you that you wouldn't win, Renee. I always win." He smiled.

"Why?" a voice whispered. That voice was hoarse and sick. That voice was mine.

"Why? What do you mean: 'why?' These people killed me! They let my body hang for four days while they pampered my mother to a funeral! When they did take me down they threw me in a pine box and sent me down a river!"

"They didn't do that. Their ancestors did—"

"And they should be punished!"

"You killed your Mother," I kept my voice soft and calm. I kept it that way to keep from shrieking. I kept it that way to keep from bursting out in tears.

"Yes, yes, I did. She tried to take away my power. She put a poison in my drink to take away my dark powers!" he argued like a little wounded kid.

"She only wanted you to be pure." That's what a mother does. They only try to help.

"Pure! She wasn't any purer than I am." He stared at me with those black eyes. Yes he'd killed his own blood, but I could see it his way. The people had no right to do what they did. It was horrible and awful and wrong. But just like they didn't have any right to do that, he didn't have any right to do this. "These people," he looked to the fiery mess of a town, "are disgusting. They deserve this."

I shook my head. He didn't understand. Even after all those years to brood over it he didn't understand. Instead he spent his time filling his only son's head with blackness. He spent his endless time planning and plotting and waiting.

"And you helped them," he breathed. He reached down and took Aria by the hair. She stood up. Her face showed nothing. "Who first, Renee?!" he thundered. "You or her?" he slid his hand along Aria's cheek. I saw her close her eyes and choke back the bile that rose in her throat from his touch. "Do you watch her die first or do you make her watch you die?!"

But he didn't let me pain over the choice. He didn't wait for the crying that would go on between my sister and me. He didn't wait for the time where I would have to choose. He threw Aria on the ground and tore of a piece of wood from his house. He stepped on one end. The old wood snapped and made a jagged point on one side.

In panic I through a blast of energy at him but he waved it off as if it had been snowflakes. He came at me with the wood and I accepted my death then. I knew it was no use in trying to move. I let him roar as he ran those few yards to where the wood would splinter through my chest. I almost wanted to fall to the ground and wait for the darkness to consume me for eternity. I almost couldn't wait to join Maria and watch over the town. Maybe this would give Aria enough time to run back to the safety of our friends.

Samuel thrust the wood at me but I didn't feel it. I opened my eyes as Rick stepped in front of Samuel. With a wave of power much like my own early on in our battle he sent Samuel banging back into his old house. Rick grabbed my hand and pulled me further behind him.

Aria smiled gratefully at him with blood stained lips.

I squeezed his hand and held back tears.

Samuel glared at him with a look that could kill. When I got up I was sure that he was going to try to kill Rick for stopping him. Instead his hand lit with fire though his flesh did not burn. He thrust his hand through Aria's chest. Her mouth dropped open and she looked at me one last time. Her eyes rolled back and when Samuel removed his hand my angel fell to the ground. In that moment I was deaf in shock. I had nothing to lose anymore. *Everything* was gone.

I screamed and tried to run for her but Rick's arms came around me. I thrashed against him and almost broke lose but he renewed his grip on me. I screamed and cried out and called the demon every unladylike word I could imagine and more.

As Aria left her body I remembered everything she'd done for me. I could remember when we were kids and she stole back my crayons. I remembered when she'd been kind enough to share her cookie with me. I remembered how we'd soothed each other through every bad moment when our parents couldn't understand. I'd confided in her when I liked Thomas and the other boys and she'd kept the secret. We'd held each other when our parents died. We'd watched out for each other ever since then.

I remembered how I wanted to take her to a place of peace when this was all over. I wanted her lay in a meadow of wild flowers and watched the clouds in the sky roll lazily by. I wanted her to be happy.

Her face filled my mind. It was her face when she was smiling. I heard the tinkling of her laughter in my ears.

I thrashed against Rick's hold and spat at Samuel as his laughter overtook Aria's.

She filled my head. I saw how she'd gone to die for me and how she'd begged me to go. I saw her pale face while she was in pain. I saw how her lips and cheeks were colorless and how she shook with exhaustion. I saw how she stood there and took everything for me. And I saw her face as she died. Her innocent face was wide with pain. I watched my angel die over and over again in my head.

Tears filled my vision. I kicked and scratched for Rick to let me go but he didn't. I shifted and slipped out of his unready arms. I rushed at Samuel and changed back. I through every sort of power I had at him. When I knocked him down I got on him and started to beat at him as I'd watched many boys do at school. He blasted me off and grabbed his stake like weapon.

This time when Rick interfered I saw the wood go through him and stick out his back. His eyes were fading out but he pushed Samuel back. With the wood still lodged in his chest he hit Samuel with weak bursts of energy.

Samuel was horrified. It didn't hurt him a bit and he waved them off easily. It was the sight of Rick fighting him even in death. As Rick started to tilt to the ground I caught him. I laid him down gently and kissed his bloody lips. I felt his last breath go out. His eyes stared up at me, open and empty. I laid my hands on his chest and actually felt his soul leave his body as his heart stuttered one last time. I cried the tears I'd been holding back since Father died. I cried them all for my two fallen angels. I closed his eyes and for a split second remembered everything.

I didn't know that I could remember so much in one night. I didn't know I could do so much in so little time. I didn't know it was possible, but I did.

I remembered the first time I'd seen him and even then I'd loved him. I remembered his loyalty to Jacob when he'd had his vision. I remembered how he'd protected me in the form of a coyote. I didn't know it was him, but it was and it comforted me now.

It took my breath away when I remembered how he wouldn't let me go alone into my own mind. He had been so kind and expected nothing in return. I felt his lips on mine and his emotions echoing back to me in the darkness. I remembered how gentle and selfless he was. He'd helped me so much in the short time I'd been here.

And Samuel was such a contrast. He was dark and disgusting with no good memories left. I doubt he knew joy anymore. He wasn't passionate; he was obsessed. Possessed. The devil incarnated.

My heart died there with him in that vile garden, just as Aria's had died with Luke. I sent myself away with Rick. I sighed and stood as Samuel was cringed against the wall of his home. He stared at Rick in awe and in disgust. The good inside of Rick was too much for Samuel to understand. Why would someone give their life for another? How could one fight after all of that? He knew it took a certain kind of person to do that. He knew it was rare to find that type of person.

For a moment all of the blackness faded from his dark eyes. For a moment he understood the love Rick and I had shared, and how no matter what happened, that love would never be broken. For a moment he understood how someone could be so selfless.

He eyes slipped to the young girl he'd just killed.

For a moment he saw how disgusting he was. He knew he'd wronged. He looked up at what was once the home where he' played and grown up. For a moment he was afraid. The demon spirit knew all the pain he'd caused and he knew that all of this was wrong. He looked up to the sky and he knew he would never touch it. He knew only angels like Rick and Aria were able to touch the stars and run on the moon.

Only angels like Maria Lenark, his mother, could ride those shooting stars and fly along with the comets.

For a moment I hoped this would be the end of it. He would change and disappear, releasing Maria, and ending this madness.

But his looked changed in that instant. It became a look of denial. Those few seconds of absolute innocence slipped away. The darkness filled his eyes and hardened his crude heart all over again. His look cursed the angels and the skies. His looked denied any part of happiness that house had brought him. He denied that he'd ended Aria's life wrongly. He denied that he'd ended a young love. The look on his face let me know that he didn't regret the burning city or the crying people as they just started this way.

He stood and brushed off his dark apparel. He turned on his nasty smile and peeled more wood from the crumbling shack behind him. He was calm and sure about this.

I stood there shaking in sadness and anger. He'd taken the last things I'd had. Without them I could walk off the edge of the earth. I could venture the land of death and not regret that choice. I just had one thing to do before I departed from this disgusting place.

"I will kill you." I said it plainly.

"We shall see, Renee," he tested the point on his stake.

I looked back to see the roses were still inching forward eager for all the blood that had been poured on to this Godforsaken ground.

I looked back to my demon and he met my eyes. We were both still . . . then he tossed to wood at me like a spear. I dodged it and slung my magic at him. We danced. We took hits and threw our own in revenge and rage. My shoulder hurt now and a cut above my eyes bled along with the one Meagan had made. Samuel clutched his leg and wiped the blood from his mouth.

He leaped for me. I was knocked to the ground and as he stood above me he made his mistake. He took a moment to take in the sight of my bleeding and bruised body. He looked at my pathetic dying scene.

He hesitated.

I had used every bit of magic I had left in my body . . . but it wasn't enough. I was losing and slipping away in exhaustion.

But I felt icy hands on my shoulders and saw Maria. I looked back to Samuel but he couldn't see her. I felt her pass all of her magic to me—and there was a lot. I was filled with it to the point where I thought I would burst. As the last trickle of her power passed into me I saw Maria smile and fade.

She could finally rest with her children that waited for her among the heavens.

As Samuel hesitated, I pulled all of my power together and pushed it out to him. His eyes grew big as he felt my energy come to him. He flew against his house with a deafening thud. I watched as the rest of the chimney fell from the roof and bits of wood and shingle fall with it. I watched as it consumed Samuel.

I looked, still lying on the ground, back to where the red roses were still creeping to me. They were so close that I would have to reach out and then I could almost touch them. Why were they still moving? Samuel was dead and they should all stop. But they kept coming closer. Maybe this place was doomed to suffer Samuel's curse for the rest of eternity.

They should let it burn. All those people that were getting closer to the house should just let it burn. It would make the blackness go away.

I heard rubble shift as I lay on my back and thought all of this. I gave the roses a glance. Only a few more inches to go. I turned my head and saw Samuel's head and arm poking out of the mess. With his last breath he sent the rest of his energy to finish off my dying body.

I flinched on the ground and before my head was slung back to watch the roses consume me I saw Samuel drift off in smoke.

Blood started to cover my vision but I could still see the hurrying figures in the distance. I saw Jacob and Drew jump the fence and I could see that Brandon wasn't far behind.

I reached back and put my hand in my lost lover's limp one. That would be how I go. I would be near Rick and Aria. I would be with my angels.

I could feel the roses against my body and one was right in front of my eye—the one that wasn't yet blinded by my own blood. They stopped moving as everything else started to go black. As I breathed shallowly the black flesh-like covering of their leaves and stems fell off. Underneath it was a beautiful bright green like none I'd ever seen. The grass around me started to grow with the same color. The moon above grew brighter and allowed me to see a little better, though it didn't last very long. As I closed my eyes to lay to rest and be in peace I saw the red drip off of the roses and leave behind a pure, glossy white.

I PROMISED

I left that world in a way I couldn't have asked for. My young Aria was near. My dear Rick lay next to me. My friends surrounded me though they could not save me, and others that I didn't even know were still on their way to help.

Before I died I had been in a dark tunnel with no beginning and no end. I had been lost in the depths of darkness. Now I made it through that tunnel.

Where I was I couldn't know. I knew it was wonderful and that was all.

A blanket of undisturbed snow fell delicately over full, green trees. Spring bloomed flowers poked through the snow and their fragrance filled the air. The sun above was warm on my skin but had no effect on the whiteness around me. Birds sang in the trees and flew overhead.

I walked through the snow, leaving no footprints to mark where I had been. The snow lightened and soon I was walking through sweet grass that glowed as it swayed in a light wind that played with my hair. Ahead was a meadow.

Wild flowers grew as far as my eyes could see. Their colors painted a scene before me that could only come from one of my mother's fairy tales. Butterflies and bees rest on their soft petals as birds sang cheerfully.

I breathed in the peace of the air and closed my eyes as I walked into the meadow. When I opened my eyes I knew I was in a sort of heaven.

I smiled as I knew I kept my promise.

Aria pranced towards me through the flowers and I heard her laughter. I'd given her a place to rest, despite how it happened. She was in a place where roses grew in the winter and the sky never grayed.

She stopped and smiled to me as she was joined by my mother and father. Others sat up in the knee-deep meadow. Others came from behind trees and appeared from nowhere.

I was sad to see them here, knowing that they had died just like me, but it was nice to know they had found their way here instead of staying behind. Barbara, Luke and Kari were all there. Smiling faces were all around me as they welcomed me as the last one to make it here, the last one to make it *home*.

I looked down to where I should have seen ground but I only saw my old world. I saw Drew and Jacob and Brandon huddled about the three bodies they had collected: Aria's, Rick's, and my own. They looked back up to me with red eyes and wet faces as if they felt my stare from somewhere in the sky.

I looked back up when I felt a warm hand close around my own. Rick stood there waiting to silently embrace me and I let him.

I had always forced myself to believe that there was something after death but in all my imaginings I never knew that I could run on the moon and ride shooting stars as the world continued on below.